D1576152

SWING LOW,
SWEET CHARIOT

ALSO IN THE SHADY GROVE
MYSTERY SERIES
Down by the Riverside
Jacob's Ladder

ALSO BY JACKIE LYNN,
WRITING AS LYNNE HINTON

FICTION
Friendship Cake
Hope Springs
Forever Friends
The Things I Know Best
The Last Odd Day
The Arms of God

NONFICTION
Meditations for Walking

SWING LOW, SWEET CHARIOT

JACKIE LYNN

ST. MARTIN'S MINOTAUR

NEW YORK

SWING LOW, SWEET CHARIOT. Copyright © 2008 by Jackie Lynn. All rights reserved. Printed in the United States of America. For information, address St. Martin's Press, 175 Fifth Avenue, New York, N.Y. 10010.

www.minotaurbooks.com

Library of Congress Cataloging-in-Publication Data

Lynn, Jackie.
    Swing low, sweet chariot: a Shady Grove mystery / Jackie Lynn.—1st ed.
        p. cm.
    ISBN-13: 978-0-312-37681-9
    ISBN-10: 0-312-37681-2
    1. Franklin Rose, (Fictitious character)—Fiction.   2. Divorced women—
Fiction.   3. Camp sites, facilities, etc.—Fiction.   4. Arkansas—Fiction.
I. Title.

PS3612.Y547S95 2008
813'.6—dc22   2008011566

First Edition: July 2008

10 9 8 7 6 5 4 3 2 1

FOR MY FRIENDS AT

FIRST CONGREGATIONAL UNITED CHURCH OF CHRIST,

RAPID CITY, SOUTH DAKOTA

ACKNOWLEDGMENTS

I gratefully acknowledge the wonderful editors at St. Martin's with whom I work, Nichole Argyres, Kylah McNeill, and the fabulous copyeditor Sabrina Soares Roberts. And, as always, thank you, Sally. You are my bright and shining star.

Swing low,
Sweet chariot,
Coming for to carry me home.
Swing low,
Sweet chariot,
Coming for to carry me home.

SWING LOW, SWEET CHARIOT

ONE

Chariot Stevens dropped her head on the steering wheel and closed her eyes. She was lost. Parked alongside State Highway 14, she was trying to figure out where she could cross back over the Missouri River and head south. She had stopped at an old turnoff that was really nothing more than just a picnic table and a parking space. She was, however, able to back the car off of the road and remain out of sight behind two large side-by-side city Dumpsters while she tried to figure out what to do next. The sun was just beginning to rise and a faint pink light emerged across the eastern sky; the prairie, flat and wide, stretched behind, in front, and all around her. A dusting of snow covered everything and Chariot looked out of the window and felt disoriented. Nothing seemed familiar. Nothing was right.

Chariot flipped on the radio, thinking that hearing the sound of talk-show hosts or early-morning disc jockeys might help with the feeling of homelessness she was suddenly facing.

She listened to a news report recorded earlier that day. Maxine Dilliard, a senator from her hometown of Mitchell, was talking about her push to stop drug trafficking in South Dakota and her efforts to shut down the meth labs taking over the plains state. Chariot turned the radio off. The chatter was not helpful.

Chariot left Pierre, South Dakota, in such a hurry that she hadn't even had a chance to study a map and it had been a long time since she had ever thought to go this far from home. When she turned out of Pierre, heading toward Holabird, she figured that there was a map in the backseat of the car and she would find a place to pull it out and read it. Once she finally did have the opportunity to stop and look in the seat pockets and the glove compartment, however, she could not find one.

The young woman leaned back against the seat and thought about where she was, what she was doing, how much she was messing things up by leaving town. She took in a long breath and considered the idea that maybe she should turn around, drive back to town, go to the police, and tell them what she knew, try to figure out everything that had happened in the last couple of hours, but she shook her head at the idea. She was too scared. Watching Jason die right in front of her was terrifying. And the way he had told her to get out of town sounded too desperate. She hated what would happen to her once she drove away and what she would lose, but she was terribly afraid of what would happen to her if she returned to Pierre.

Chariot glanced around in the car. She was relieved to see that she had the necessary supplies for camping. Jason had thought to pack the tent and sleeping bags. He had already made sure to take the blankets off of the bed, throw them in the backseat, and box up bottled water, peanut butter, chips, and crackers. He had loaded the car with everything they would need to get lost and stay missing. Chariot had what she needed to leave South Dakota. She just didn't know why she had to leave, why Jason had insisted that she grab her things and get ready to go in the wee hours of the morning. She didn't know where he was planning to drive them and now that she was alone, she didn't know where she was going.

It had all happened so fast. When she woke up, he was standing over her, shaking her, and he told her only that she needed to get up and get ready, that he had already gathered up some of her clothes, but that she needed to figure out what else she might need for a trip. Half-asleep and still lost in a dream filled with laughing children, she had asked him what was wrong and where they were going and he had said only that they had to go right away, that they had to get out of the apartment at that very moment, and that he would explain it all once they were out of town.

He told her to get out of bed and put on her clothes, the ones he had thrown on the chair in the bedroom, the ones she now had on. He said that she had a few minutes to gather as much as she could and not to worry about what she couldn't take, that money wasn't a problem and they would buy clothes and extra stuff later. He assured her that even though it looked bad at that moment, everything was going to be fine, that she just needed to do what he said and to trust him.

Chariot refused at first. She didn't want to leave Pierre. She had made a home for herself there. She said she wasn't going to go, couldn't go, but in the end she did what he asked. She listened to his instructions, heard the desperation in his voice, and she followed them. He hated doing this, he had said, and he promised her that he would make it right.

She threw on her jeans and the navy blue sweater that he had picked out for her. She pulled on her hiking boots and stuffed a duffel bag with her makeup and purse and underwear. She grabbed as much of her jewelry as she could and she managed to find the tiny pair of yellow ceramic boots that her grandmother had given her when she was a child. She added her stuffed teddy bear won at the county fair, a box of toys, and a few baby clothes she had been saving. She threw in a few CDs, a photo album, the picture she kept by her bed of a baby wrapped in a thin pink blanket, and the birth certificate in the bedside table. She didn't have time to get anything else.

Jason rushed her out to the car with her arms full. He handed her the keys and told her to start the engine and try to scrape the windshield while he packed a few more things from his desk. She followed his instructions without questioning him because she could see that something was wrong, something was causing Jason to push her to leave quickly. She could only trust him.

She found the car exactly where he had said it would be, not in their usual spot in front of the apartment unit, but behind in the alley, next to a tall chain-link fence. She hurried over to it, found the door unlocked, and piled her things on top of the stuff already in the backseat. As she tried to get the car started, she heard the distant sound of a motorcycle and noticed that it seemed to be coming toward the front of the apartment.

It took ten minutes to crank the engine of the car. It was an old Plymouth, one Jason had when she met him; they had often laughed that it had a mind of its own, especially in the winter. Finally, after a number of tries, the engine started, and Chariot revved the motor and turned on the heat. She got out and tried to clear the windshield with a piece of old cardboard she found on the floorboard. There had been a late spring snowstorm early in the night and everything was covered in three or four inches of the large wet flakes.

She scraped as much as she could, shivering in the cold and dark, and wondered how long her boyfriend had been awake before he had gotten her out of bed, how long he had known they were going to leave Pierre. She wondered how she would explain things to the parole officer and the manager of the diner. She wondered how she would ever recover what she was sure that she was losing.

She slid the cardboard from side to side across the icy windshield and figured that once again everything in her life was falling apart. Once again, just when she thought things were going to be fine, that she was finally going to have a normal and happy life, something was happening to bring her down. Something Jason had done was going to take away everything she had worked so hard to achieve.

She cleared the windshield and reached into the car and turned on the wipers. She threw the cardboard over the fence and headed back toward her apartment, heading back to tell Jason that she couldn't go, that he was going to have to take care of things himself. And then she saw someone coming out of the front door. She didn't get a good look at his face, but he reminded her of men she had seen before. There was something familiar, she thought, about the way he walked, the way he glanced around, always watching, the way he stepped with authority.

He was tall, had a silver helmet on his head, and was wearing a thick black leather jacket. He was dressed in dark clothes, with tall black leather boots. He hadn't noticed her because when Chariot saw him, she moved away from the light and stood against the building. When Chariot heard the motorcycle start up and when she thought that he was gone, she stepped out into the light.

Chariot carefully glanced around in all directions and, seeing no one else, quickly ran to her apartment. She looked in the den and kitchen and finally down the hallway. That was where she saw him. Jason was crumpled on the floor. Blood was splattered across the walls. She made her way over to him and knelt beside him, trying to see if he was still breathing. He opened his eyes just as she pressed her fingers against his neck. She was just about to jump up and dial 911. But with his last breath, he grabbed her and pulled her to him.

"Go!" he said, his voice only a harsh whisper. "They think you're at work, the graveyard shift. They're going there now because they think you've got it. You've got to go now. I'm sorry, Chariot, I didn't know it would turn out like this. Just don't"—his voice fell away—"president . . ." And then he released his grip on her collar and collapsed.

"Jason!" she screamed his name. "Jason!"

Chariot felt for his pulse again and found none. She thought again to call 911, to get an ambulance, to get the police. She wanted to get help for Jason and for her, but she felt paralyzed, frozen. She knew that calling the authorities would be the smart thing to do, but she was torn because of what Jason had said. There was something about the way he warned her with his last breath, something about the way he had pulled her from her sleep that night, something even about the way he had acted all week that made her know she needed to do what he had said.

She was still kneeling next to Jason when she heard the motorcycle making the turn a few blocks from the apartment. She shook her head, gave Jason one last look, and ran out of the front door and got in the car. She backed out of the alley and began speeding down the side road that eventually intersected with the state highway. She hoped that she hadn't been noticed by anyone, especially the man on the approaching motorcycle, and she drove the seventeen miles that led to Highway 83. She went past the turnoff for the highway and headed toward Miller.

Chariot drove without stopping. She kept watching the rearview mirror, but didn't see anyone following her. She hurried along Highway 14, heading east. She thought she'd get to Huron, about an hour and half away, and then call the police there. If she was able to get to the next town without being seen by the murderer maybe she'd be safe. She'd tell them everything she knew, including a description of the man she saw leaving the apartment, the man who had killed Jason.

Chariot drove until the sun started to rise. Finally, stopping at the little makeshift rest stop near Lake Louise, she stopped to find the map and to catch her breath. Checking her gas gauge, she saw that there was almost a half a tank. Thinking she would make it to the town with that, Chariot knew that she could get gas when she stopped to make the call in Huron. Everything would work out then. She figured she would make it there just as the main office at the police station opened and she would explain what she had seen, describe the man who killed Jason. She took a deep breath, resolved at what she had to do, and was just about to pull out from behind the Dumpsters when she saw the motorcycle speed past. She slammed on the brakes.

Chariot felt her pulse quicken. She knew the man on the motorcycle was the killer. She recognized him from the apartment. She could see right away the broad shoulders and the black jacket, the silver helmet, and the long black boots. Jason had warned her that they would be looking for her. She knew that he was now after her. But now, there was something even more troublesome about her situation, something she had not noticed or seen before. She was stunned by what she saw on the motorcycle as it sped past.

Flashing across the front fender of the murderer's bike was a panel of state-issued blue lights. The man who murdered Jason and the man who was after Chariot drove a police motorcycle. Suddenly, everything she had just planned was wiped away. The police were somehow involved. She wasn't going to be able to contact any law enforcement officer now, not even in Huron. She turned back in the direction she had come, then headed south on the first highway she found.

TWO

But I don't know how to dance." Rose had stopped by Ms. Lou Ellen's before heading over to the office to open up for business. Mary, the manager of Shady Grove Campground, had taken the week off to visit a sister who had just arrived in the States from their home country of Vietnam. Rose was in charge of the office while her friend was away.

"Darling, no one really knows *how* to dance, one simply dances." Ms. Lou Ellen, who lived in the cabin right across the driveway from the campground office, was trying to persuade Rose to go to the Spring Fling Dance that was being held in West Memphis later in the month. She was selling tickets to benefit St. Jude's Hospital, which was just across the bridge in Memphis.

"Just instruct Thomas to take his dark Sunday suit to Fiore's for cleaning, buy you a pink flower over at Judith's Florist, and escort you to a decent social outing. Once you hear the music playing, the dancing will simply happen." Ms. Lou Ellen was pouring herself a cup of tea. "Besides, it's in your horoscope. Would you like some ginger spice?" she asked.

Rose shook her head. "I've got to get the coffee going at the office, but I will take a biscuit." She knew Ms. Lou Ellen always had something baked for breakfast. During the time she had been working at Shady Grove, Rose always enjoyed stopping for breakfast at Ms. Lou Ellen's. "A dance is in my horoscope?" she asked. She knew that her friend followed astrology and studied the charts of everyone she knew.

"Of course," the older woman responded, reaching for a plate for Rose. "A social event is expected for you in this new season. And yes, we must make sure we have coffee for our campers," she noted with a smile.

"That's your son-in-law's motto," Rose added, referring to Lucas Boyd who was married to Rhonda, Lou Ellen's daughter. They were the owners of Shady Grove Campground and hospitality was their key policy. She took a bite of biscuit.

"Yes," Lou Ellen responded. "Free coffee and a picturesque spot on the river." She sipped her tea. "What more could a person need camping along the Mississippi?"

"Not much," Rose replied. "This is, after all, the finest riverbank campground in West Memphis, Arkansas." She wiped her mouth. "You are going to have to teach me how to bake a decent biscuit."

"Of course, dear, it is the only riverbank campground in West Memphis, Arkansas. And why would you want to learn to bake a biscuit when I am baking them for you?"

Rose smiled. "You're right. And regarding campgrounds, even if there was another, I bet Shady Grove would outdo them."

"In a flash," Ms. Lou Ellen noted. "Now, back to the Spring Fling debate."

Rose sighed. "I'm not debating it. Look, I'll buy a couple of tickets if you need to sell them, but I'm not sure that a dance at the VFW will be something Tom or I will attend. Besides, he has escorted me to a decent social outing."

"It's the Elks," Ms. Lou Ellen noted.

"What?" Rose asked, sounding confused. She ate her last bite and got up to place the plate in the sink.

"The Spring Fling, it's at the Elks Lodge, not the VFW." She put down her cup of tea. "I don't think the veterans honor spring with a fling."

"But the Elks do?" Rose asked, going over to the refrigerator to pour herself a glass of juice and then sitting back down at the table.

"In grand style," Ms. Lou Ellen replied. "And taking you to the RV and Camping Show at the Coliseum isn't really what I'd call a formal affair," she added.

Rose rolled her eyes. She drank the juice. "We've been dressed up together."

Ms. Lou Ellen glanced over at her friend. "Yes?" she asked and then put down her cup and interlaced her fingers together, placing her hands in front of her on the table. "Name me a time."

Rose cleared her throat and put down the glass. "We've been to a jazz club on Beale Street once. Tom wore a jacket. And we go out to dinner at least once a month." She folded her arms across her chest. "We do stuff," she protested, wiping her mouth.

"Yes," Ms. Lou Ellen noted. "I know all about your stuff." She winked.

Rose blushed. "Okay, look, just to get you off of my back, I will purchase two tickets for the Grand Elks annual Spring Fling."

"Great, we can go to Anne Marie's shop in Memphis to find you an appropriate dress to wear." Ms. Lou Ellen had put on her reading glasses and began looking at a calendar that was close to her, by the phone. "How does next Thursday look for you?"

"I said that I would buy the tickets. I didn't say I would use them." Rose got up from the table and took a long stretch. "Besides, I have a dress."

Ms. Lou Ellen turned to face Rose, her reading glasses halfway down her nose. She peered at her friend in disbelief. "You have a dress?"

Rose nodded, ready to make her exit. "Yes," she replied, then glanced over again to see Lou Ellen's look of surprise. "What? You don't believe that I have a dress?" Rose asked.

"Oh, I believe you might have had a dress in your past, but I have visited your little camper, remember? And the only thing I've seen hanging on a hanger is a pale green jacket." She closed the calendar and took another sip of her tea.

Rose knew that Ms. Lou Ellen couldn't imagine a person living in a small travel trailer like the one Rose was in. She had often questioned Rose about how she stood such a small space. Rose had always answered her truthfully. She had never minded. She had discovered that she really didn't need much to live and she was happy not to have to clean or manage a house. The fiberglass camper was more than enough room for one person. Besides, when she felt cramped she always went to visit her friends.

"No, it's not in the closet." She cleared her throat and started toward the door. "I have a couple of boxes that I haven't unpacked. They're still in the truck."

Ms. Lou Ellen raised her eyebrows and smiled. She waited until Rose had turned back around to face her. "You have a Spring Fling dress that has been folded up in a box for almost two years? Darling, don't you think it's time to unpack your bags and stay?"

Rose considered her friend's question. "Two years?" She sounded surprised. "Has it really been that long that I've been here?" Rose asked.

It seemed to her like it had only been a few weeks since she had packed up the travel trailer and her vehicle and left Rocky Mount, North Carolina. Her husband had left her for another woman. She and her brother had placed her father in a nursing home and he had since died. She had known that she could get a job as a nurse anywhere in the country so she had just packed up and left.

At the time she had only known that she was heading west, leaving the only life she had ever known and going on an adventure. And although, she traveled west for a number of hours, she hadn't gotten nearly as far as she had expected. She had never expected to stay in West Memphis. She was going to Arizona or

New Mexico, maybe even California. Stopping in Arkansas and staying at a campground for more than twenty months had been a surprise to everyone who knew her, but it was a bigger surprise to Rose herself. And more, she had not expected to find what she did at the Shady Grove Campground. She had found home.

"I believe the day of your arrival was the day they found the body of Lawrence Franklin. And I'm quite certain the first anniversary of his funeral has come and gone. In fact, it is almost the second year of his passing." Ms. Lou Ellen took off her glasses.

Rose nodded. She remembered the day she got to Shady Grove. Her SUV had broken down. The mechanic had told her that it was going to take a few days to get the parts. She was planning to stay at the river campground for only the time it took to get her vehicle repaired before resuming her western adventure. Once the vehicle was fixed, however, she had stayed for several reasons.

She stayed because she had become involved in the investigation of the drowning victim. She stayed because she fell in love with Thomas Sawyer. And she stayed because of the friendships she made—with Mary, the Vietnamese woman who ran Shady Grove and taught her the importance of honesty and loyalty; with Lucas and Rhonda, the evangelical bikers who welcomed her like she was family; and especially with Ms. Lou Ellen, a woman who doled out wisdom in short, pithy sayings and generated more goodwill and kindness than Rose had ever experienced.

"It doesn't seem that long," Rose noted. "And yet, it also seems like I've been here my whole life."

Ms. Lou Ellen smiled. "I have found that the best events in life always feel that way." She took in a breath. "Unbelievably quick and unquestionably full."

The two women pondered the thought and the time that Rose had been at Shady Grove.

"Now, it is quite time for you to unpack those boxes of Spring Fling dresses that you've been hiding. And I will take a good look at the one you think is appropriate. Frankly, my dear, I would love to see you in something other than—" She nodded toward Rose, looking at her from head to toes.

Rose followed her eyes. "What's wrong with what I wear?" she asked. She thought her look was perfectly fine. After all, she was always clean and she never wore a T-shirt that didn't match her jeans or khakis. And since she started yoga, she had branched off into a new fashion genre that included a lot of stretch pants. She particularly liked that look.

"Let's just say I haven't seen a knee or a waistline since I've known you," Ms. Lou Ellen replied. "And yet, I have learned with my daughter's wardrobe, predictability can be surprisingly, well, predictable."

Rose thought about what her friend was saying. She considered Rhonda's standard outfits of leather and black and orange Harley-Davidson attire.

Rose knew that when Rhonda was a child her mother had wanted to dress her in pink bows and ruffles. She recalled hearing that by the time Rhonda was a teenager, Ms. Lou Ellen had ultimately given up on trying to turn her tomboy daughter into a little girl.

"You think I dress kind of boring?" she asked.

"Dear, you dress just fine for managing a campground, picking up the trash and raking gravel. Why, I'm sure your uniform is comfortable and easy to wash. I just think it might be nice to see you dressed up. I suspect our Thomas might enjoy that." She finished her tea. "But, I have learned my lesson from Rhonda. I needn't try to dress other women."

Rose glanced down again at her outfit. She hadn't worn anything other than jeans, khakis, and stretch pants since she had been in West Memphis. Even at Lawrence Franklin's funeral and the times she went with Rhonda and Lucas to church, she had kept her appearance very casual. She certainly knew that Thomas never cared about how she dressed, but she did wonder if he might like to see her all dolled up.

"You know, I think I will see what is in those boxes. It's been so long I don't even remember what else I brought with me." Then she reconsidered. "Or you know, maybe I might like to buy a new dress," she said as she opened the front door to leave. "Did you know that the only thing new I've bought since I got here was a couple of sets of workout clothes?"

"I would never have guessed," the older woman replied with a grin. She could hardly restrain her enthusiasm at the thought of being able to help a young woman shop. "Next Thursday we shall drive across the bridge to Tennessee and pick you out a dress for the Elks' Spring Fling."

Rose nodded. "It's a date," she agreed. "Do you think Rhonda might like to join us?" she asked.

Ms. Lou Ellen rolled her eyes. "Anne Marie does not carry chaps."

"Right," Rose noted. "So, it's just us then?"

The older woman nodded. "I suspect that will be aplenty."

"Great. Okay, now, I must take my fashion-challenged self and get this campground in working order. Otherwise, those pesky owners will have my job!" She winked at Ms. Lou Ellen and headed out the door.

"Ta-ta," the older woman said. "And ask Lester Earl to come in. His breakfast is getting cold."

Rose stepped off of the cabin porch and saw Lester Earl lying at the bottom step. The three-legged black dog had been living at Shady Grove ever since he arrived with the camper from New Mexico, Jacob Sunspeaker. Rose bent down to pet the dog and recalled how they had become acquainted. Mr. Sunspeaker had been murdered at the campground and Ms. Lou Ellen had taken the orphaned dog under her wing. Lester Earl, the name of Ms. Lou Ellen's second husband, was now as much a part of the Shady Grove family as was Rose.

"Hey, buddy," Rose said as she scratched the dog on the head and under his chin. "You want to go with me to the office or would you rather have a ham biscuit?"

The dog whined a bit and jumped up on the steps and ran to the door. He pushed it open and walked in the house. Rose could hear Ms. Lou Ellen greeting her pet.

"I guess breakfast sounds more enticing than sitting in the office with me," Rose said to herself. She headed over to the campground office.

"A new dress and a dance," she said to herself, shaking her head. "How does that woman talk me into things?"

She unlocked the door and walked inside, turning the OPEN-CLOSED sign over to reveal the word *open* and closed the door. She pulled up the blinds and walked over to the counter where the coffeepot was placed. After emptying out the filter and grounds from the previous day, she rinsed out the pot and started a fresh one. And then she headed over to the desk where Mary usually sat and began looking over the mail from the previous day that she had not gotten around to opening.

Most of it was junk, she decided, and she tossed the flyers and form letters into the trash can beside the desk. She noticed a catalogue for a local department store and began flipping through the pages. After her conversation with Ms. Lou Ellen, she was suddenly curious about the clothing styles.

When she noticed that the coffeepot was full, she got up from the desk and went over and poured herself a cup. She was returning to the desk when the phone began to ring. She sat down and picked up the receiver. "It's a beautiful day at Shady Grove," she answered cheerfully.

There was no response.

"Hello," Rose said. "Anybody there?"

Still nothing.

"Hello," Rose repeated. She was just about to hang up the phone when she heard the timid voice.

"Is this Rhonda?"

"No," Rose replied. "Rhonda doesn't usually work in the of-fice. This is Rose. Can I help?"

There was a pause.

"I need to talk to Rhonda."

"Well, I can try to find her, but I'll have to get you to call back or have her call you. I haven't seen her this morning and I don't always know where she and Lucas are." Rose wondered if they were on the premises or had taken off on one of their many mis-sion trips that they liked to make. She often had a difficult time keeping up with where they were.

"It's real important," the woman noted. "Tell her it's Chariot, Chariot Stevens," she added. "Tell her I'm in Memphis. And tell her I'm in trouble."

And then, all of a sudden, the line went dead.

THREE

"Hello, hello!" Rose kept shouting into the phone, thinking that maybe the caller was on a cell phone and just went out of range for a few seconds. She called out again and finally decided that the phone call had been disconnected.

She was trying to figure out how to get hold of Rhonda when the front door opened. It was the man from Texas who parked his fifth wheel at site sixty-three, on the other end from where Rose was hooked up.

"Good morning," he said as he closed the door behind him.

"Just in time for coffee." Rose moved toward the counter. She put on her best hospitality face.

"No, no." The man shook his head and waved his hands in front of him. "I've already had four cups this morning. I couldn't drink another sip if it was forced on me."

Rose smiled and leaned in his direction. "Well, I don't intend to force a beverage on you first thing in the morning. So, what can I do for you?" she asked. "Everything okay at your site?"

He nodded. "Ah, it's real pretty out here, ain't it?" He scratched his chin and looked out the window toward his fifth-wheel trailer. He was wearing jeans and a lightweight jacket. Rose thought he looked to be in his late seventies, probably a full-timer, the term used for those who stay in their motor homes all the time.

"Yep, everything is just fine. We've enjoyed ourselves quite a bit on the Mississippi. But the wife and I would like to take a little side trip and we were wondering if we could leave the rig for a week or so."

He turned back to Rose. "We'd move it from the river site and put it out of the way. We were just going to see if maybe we could get a reduced rate since we wouldn't exactly be here to use any of the utilities."

Rose nodded. This was not an unusual or unreasonable request. Several campers liked to park their units on the river and then head over to other places to stay with family or in hotels. Rose glanced down at the workplace on the counter and pulled out the small notebook where Mary had a written record for the discounting of prices for the kind of arrangement this man was requesting. She flipped to the right page.

"If you park over here in the woods and don't turn on the utilities, we can let you stay for twelve dollars a night," she noted. "If you stay where you are, even without the utilities, it's still going to cost you twenty-one dollars, just like you're already paying."

He considered the prices. He shifted his weight from side to side as he chewed on his lip.

Rose waited for his decision.

"You know, since we're already unhooked and we'd like to linger on a couple more days when we get back, we'll just pay the twenty-one dollars and stay where we are." He nodded his head. "I think I can afford that," he added.

"Okay," Rose responded. "You want to go ahead and pay for the week?" she asked. "And if you do that, you actually get one day free," she noted.

"Well, now, little lady, you can't beat that with a stick, can you?" He pulled out his wallet and took out a credit card. "Go ahead and charge me for six days at that rate, add on the free day, and then we'll pay for what we owe you when we get back next week."

"That'll work." Rose took the man's card and ran it through the machine. Then she wrote down in the reservation book that the site was reserved. "So, how long should I keep your spot reserved?" she asked.

The man thought about the question. "I'd say ten days," he replied. "That gives us a week to take care of our trip and then get back and stay a couple more nights before heading back home." He slid his hands in his pants pockets. "Is that okay?" he asked.

"That's fine," Rose replied, making a note in the book for the ten-day reservation. She finished writing it down and closed the book. "Are you going into Tennessee for your trip?" she asked.

"What?" the man asked, appearing a bit confused by Rose's question.

The credit card machine spat out the receipt and Rose pulled it out and placed it on the counter for the man to sign. She handed him back his credit card and then put the amount in the cash register, a separate procedure.

"Your side trip?" Rose explained. "You said that you were leaving the camper because you and your wife were taking a side trip."

The man took his card and put it back in his wallet.

"But never mind," Rose said. "I didn't mean to pry."

He took the pen on the counter and signed the receipt. "No, that's all right," he said, taking his copy. "I don't consider it prying. The side trip isn't to Tennessee."

"Oh," Rose responded, not sure that she should ask anything else. She rang up the transaction, took the receipt, and placed it in the open cash register. Then she closed the cash drawer.

"We're going up around Jonesboro, up near the Missouri border," the Texan said. "My wife's people, they're from Paragould." He thought for a moment. "Well, not Paragould really, more west of that, Walnut Ridge is where we think."

"Where you think?" Rose couldn't help herself. "You don't know for sure?" She had gotten nosier since she had moved to Shady Grove.

The man shook his head. "Kathryn is seventy years old and she never knew where she came from."

Rose waited.

The man continued. "She was given to a family from Dallas when she was only a baby and she just grew up never asking anything." He glanced out the window toward his camper and truck. "Suddenly, she's interested in finding her folks," he noted.

He turned back to Rose. "Our granddaughter started asking questions for some college course she was taking and it just stirred up the past for Kathryn. So, I promised her last fall that I would bring her down here and we'd poke around. She found out some things, like Jonesboro, from some computer program our granddaughter put her on." He fidgeted with the zipper on his jacket. "I told her it was silly, but I reckon she's made up her mind about this."

Rose listened. She smiled at the man. "I think you're doing a very good thing," she said.

The man studied her. "What makes you think that?" he asked, narrowing his eyes at her.

Rose felt him watching her as she prepared to answer. She wondered if she had offended the campground guest. She shrugged her shoulders. "Your wife wants to find out stuff about her past, her family, answer some questions she's probably had in her mind a long time. You're helping her do that. You're helping her answer some very important questions," Rose noted.

The man blew out a breath and scratched his chin again. "I don't know," he said, drawing out the words. "I think asking a lot of questions about the past doesn't bring about any answers; it just causes more questions."

Rose leaned against the counter. The sun was shining through the window and she could see the river from where she stood. "Nothing wrong with questions," she noted. "I've learned that."

The man grinned, softening a bit. "You sound just like my granddaughter," he responded.

Rose laughed.

"You have children?" he asked.

Rose hadn't been asked that question in a long time. "No," she replied, and gave no further answer.

The man decided not to press her. "Well, the wife is going to do what she wants to do anyway. It doesn't matter what I think," he added. "After all, we're here now and we might as well do what we set out to do. We'll head up north and maybe she'll find something that makes her feel better."

"I think you're wrong about that," Rose said.

The man appeared a bit confused.

"I think it matters a lot about what you think," she explained. "And I think that you must love your wife and granddaughter a lot to follow through on this. And I think you'll find that the fact you're willing to help her ask her questions will turn out to be the most important answer your wife gets."

Rose reached behind her and got her cup of coffee. She noticed how it had grown cold since she had engaged in the conversation. She raised the cup. "You sure you don't want a cup to go?" she asked.

"Nah," he replied. "I had aplenty. I guess I better get back to the rig."

"Anything else I can help you with?" Rose asked.

"Well, since you asked, I might pose one question to you. Where's the county courthouse around here?"

"Downtown West Memphis," Rose replied. "Which office you looking for and I'll look them up in the phone book, tell you exactly where it is?"

The man shook his head. "I don't even know," he answered. "I got a question about the state of Arkansas, child and family services would answer it, I guess." He folded his arms across his chest. He waited.

"Well, what's the question? Maybe I can help you figure out who to ask." Rose was curious.

"We're trying to figure out if the state will tell you who your birth parents are, trying to find out if they'll tell you who gave you away."

Rose made a humming noise. She had never thought of that question before. She knew she didn't have the answer. "Well, that's a new one for me," she admitted. "But if you want me to, I can certainly find out for you," she added. "I'll make a few calls and let you know something when you get back."

The man smiled. "I'd appreciate that. Well, I better run. Kathryn's probably wondering what happened to me. We got a lot to do before we head out."

Rose nodded as the man opened the door to leave.

"It's been nice talking to you," he noted. He turned around to face her again. "By the way, how did you get so smart about married folks?" he asked. "I noticed you don't wear a ring."

Rose looked down at her finger. She had been without her wedding band for almost two years. She shook her head and glanced back up at the man standing at the door. "I used to be married," she replied. "And I'm not so smart about it," she added with a confessional tone.

He stood in the doorway and grinned. "You expect it would have been different if he had let you ask your questions?"

"I expect it would have been different if he had asked his own," she replied. "But then, I don't know that anything would have changed no matter what questions we would have asked. Truth is, we're both better off not married to each other."

The man seemed to think about the response. He looked in her direction and nodded his head. Then he lifted his hand and waved, turned, and walked out the door.

Rose watched as he headed down the driveway toward the river sites. She walked over and threw out the cup of cold coffee down the sink and poured herself another cup. She wondered about the man from Texas and his wife, wondered what they would find in Walnut Ridge, wondered about the questions that the woman was asking. She thought about the man's willingness to help his wife revisit her past and she was warmed by the man's tenderness.

She was refilling her cup, considering the conversation she had just had when she remembered the phone call she had received before the man came into the office. She hurried back over to the desk and dialed Rhonda's cell phone. Rose wasn't sure where Rhonda was, but she assumed that she would have her cell phone.

Rhonda answered on the second ring.

"Rhonda, it's Rose."

"Well, good morning. What's up?" she asked. "You in the office?"

"Yeah," Rose replied. "Mary is still with her sister."

"Right."

"Hey, I didn't want to bother you, but you just had a phone

call a few minutes ago. I was going to call you right after it came through, but a camper came in. Anyway, it was someone who said her name was Charity or Cherry." Rose was having difficulty remembering the caller's name. "She said she was a friend of yours and that she was in Memphis and that she was in trouble." That part she remembered. That part had been clearly stated.

"Charity?" Rhonda asked.

There was a pause.

"I don't know anybody by that name. Did she say her last name?"

Rose tried to think about the phone call she had received. "No, just Charity." She thought again. "No, wait, it was Chariot, like the song."

"What song?" Rhonda asked.

" 'Swing Low, Sweet Chariot,' " Rose replied.

"Oh."

Another pause.

"Chariot?" she repeated. "I don't know a Chariot, either."

"Well, hopefully, she'll call back and I can find out more," Rose responded.

"Chariot," Rhonda said again. She was trying to figure out the identity of the caller. "In Memphis."

"In trouble," Rose added.

"Right."

"I could star 69 her," Rose thought aloud.

"Is that something illegal?" Rhonda asked.

Rose laughed. "No, it's not illegal."

"Does it hurt?" she asked.

"No," Rose responded. "I dial star 69 and it gives me the number of the last party who called."

Rose had read about it in the office phone features booklet that Mary had given her when she was learning how to take messages and put the phone on a forwarding feature so that it would ring on the mobile unit.

"Well, try it and then call me back," Rhonda responded. "We're just outside Greenville, Mississippi. We stopped to gas up."

Rose listened and she could hear the sounds of traffic on the other end. She realized that it was lucky that she was able to reach her boss since there was no way Rhonda could hear the phone ring while she was driving her motorcycle.

"I won't leave until I hear from you," Rhonda added.

"Okay."

"Lucas says hey," Rhonda said. "What's Mama doing today?"

"Hey to Lucas. And she's trying to get me to go to a dance."

"The Spring Fling?" Rhonda seemed to know what her mother was up to most of the time even if she wasn't around that much.

"That's the one," Rose replied.

"Well, at least she's given up on me and Lucas for that." Rhonda paused. "Is she going to take you shopping, too?"

"Over to Anne Marie's," answered Rose.

There was a laugh from the other end.

"Okay, look, I'll call you right back when I find out something about the call."

Rhonda was still laughing when the two of them hung up their phones.

Rose put down the receiver and dialed star 69. The recorded voice gave the date and time of the last received call. Then there was a number that Rose wrote down. She glanced over it and didn't recognize the area code of 605. She phoned Rhonda again. Her friend answered before the second ring and spoke before Rose ever had time to tell her the information she had received.

"It's Chariot Stevens," Rhonda said before Rose could give her the number. "She's from South Dakota. We met at the bike rally a number of years ago and she's almost always in trouble."

FOUR

Oh, okay," Rose replied. "Do you want me to call her back and tell her you're far away, maybe give her the address of social services?"

There was a pause on the other end of the line. Rhonda was considering Rose's suggestions.

"Nah," she finally answered. "Give me her number and I'll call her. I wouldn't turn down a friend in trouble, even one who tends to stay that way."

Rose was just about to give the number when she noticed an old Plymouth driving down the driveway in her direction. She waited as it came to a stop right in front of the office. She didn't recognize the driver. She told Rhonda to hold on and she placed the receiver on the desk and moved closer to the window. She studied the car, and since it was stopped beyond the front window, she was able to read the license plate. The car was from South Dakota.

Rose walked back over to the desk and picked up the phone again. "I don't think you have to worry about calling her. She just pulled up to the campground." .

There was a sigh.

"Well, just tell her we'll be back at Shady Grove by lunchtime. Do you mind helping her find a place to wait?" Rhonda asked.

Rose smiled. She did love her boss and friend's soft heart. "Of course," she responded. "We'll be in the office."

Rose watched as the young woman closed the car door and headed up the steps of the office. She said good-bye to Rhonda and was waiting for the visitor as she walked inside.

"Morning," she said as a way of greeting.

"Hello," the young woman replied hesitantly.

Rose could tell that she was uncomfortable. She looked around nervously. It appeared as if she hadn't slept in a number of days. Her shoulder-length brown hair was pulled up in a messy ponytail. Her clothes were wrinkled and stained, proba-bly from eating while she drove, Rose thought. Her eyes gave away her fatigue and she fidgeted as she stood just inside the door.

"Come on in," Rose added.

The woman walked toward the counter. The door shut be-hind her and she jumped a bit at the sound.

"Welcome to Shady Grove. Can I help you?" Rose decided not to let on that she knew who the visitor was, that she recog-nized her as the woman who had called Rhonda earlier.

"I'm, uh, looking for Rhonda Boyd," she replied, glancing around, trying to find some proof that she had come to the right place. "Does she still live here?" she asked, hoping the information she received was correct.

Rose nodded. "Yes, she and Lucas are the owners of Shady Grove, but they aren't here most of the time."

The girl looked disappointed. She began biting her bottom lip. She then dropped her eyes and appeared as if she had run out of ideas for herself.

"I just talked to Rhonda, though, and she and Lucas are on their way here. They should just be a couple of hours."

She looked up at Rose. She seemed relieved.

Rose studied the visitor. "Do you want a cup of coffee?" she asked, assuming the young woman needed some sustenance.

She nodded.

Rose walked over to the coffeepot, took one of Mary's mugs from the cabinet, and poured the visitor a cup. "You take anything in it?" she asked as she turned around.

She shook her head. "Just black," she replied, moving toward Rose and taking the cup from her.

"There," Rose announced as she handed over the cup. "Nothing like a cup of joe to ease the mind."

The visitor smiled and took a sip. She seemed to relax with the gift of the morning beverage and the small display of hospitality. "My name is Chariot. Chariot Stevens," she said. "I've been driving all night. I'm from South Dakota."

Rose nodded. "And I'm Rose. It's nice to meet you. Have you eaten anything?"

She shook her head again, as she drank another sip. "I had a burger about midnight," she said.

"Well, you need some breakfast," Rose responded as she walked over to the desk and picked up the phone. "Would you like a biscuit? I know where there are some freshly made this morning," she added, remembering Ms. Lou Ellen's plate of ham biscuits.

"You serve food here?" the woman asked. She glanced around looking for cooking and serving facilities.

Rose smiled. "Let me just make a call." She held the receiver in one hand and dialed Ms. Lou Ellen. She made the request, and in only a matter of minutes, the older woman was standing on the porch with two biscuits on a small plate, wrapped in a linen napkin. Rose noticed how her friend studied the car before opening the door and coming into the office.

"You're in luck," Rose announced as Ms. Lou Ellen walked through the door. "The three-legged dog didn't eat them all."

The visitor was sitting at the table and Rose was leaning against the counter. Ms. Lou Ellen arrived so quickly Rose hadn't had the chance to learn anything more about the young woman.

"Well, hello dear," Ms. Lou Ellen said, drawing out every syllable. She placed the plate in front of the guest, pulled away the napkin in grand style, and held out her hand to shake.

Chariot stood up to return the greeting, knocking over the chair behind her. "Oh, gosh, I'm sorry," she said as she reached down and picked it up. "I don't mean to be so clumsy," she added.

Ms. Lou Ellen helped her put the chair back at the table and the visitor sat down.

"No worries, child," Ms. Lou Ellen responded. She sat down

across from her. "I'm Lou Ellen Johnston Maddox Perkins," she noted as an introduction. "You can just call me Ms. Lou Ellen. And these are my ham biscuits." She smiled.

Chariot nodded. She glanced down at the food in front of her. "I'm real glad to meet you," she responded.

"I'm not sure if you mean me or the biscuits, but either way, we are delighted to make your acquaintance." Ms. Lou Ellen winked over at Rose.

"This is Chariot Stevens," Rose explained. "She's from South Dakota." Since that was all the information she had, that was all she said.

"South Dakota?" Ms. Lou Ellen repeated. "Well, that's just lovely. How is it that you're from the great state of South Dakota?"

Chariot appeared confused. "I, uh, I was just born there," she replied.

"Right," Ms. Lou Ellen said. "And we have no say in those matters, do we?" she asked with a wink.

Chariot blushed, not sure of what else to say.

"Please, enjoy!" Ms. Lou Ellen pushed the biscuits closer to the visitor from South Dakota.

Chariot began to eat. She took small bites and both Rose and Ms. Lou Ellen noticed how her hands shook as she held the biscuit. The two women glanced at each other.

"Rhonda called," Rose said as a means to divert their attention off of the young woman eating.

"Is she somewhere in this country?" Ms. Lou Ellen asked.

Chariot looked at Rose for the answer.

Ms. Lou Ellen explained as she noticed the questioning look upon the visitor's face. "Rhonda is my daughter; she sometimes goes missing."

Chariot nodded.

"She's in Greenville," Rose replied.

"Mississippi?" Ms. Lou Ellen asked.

"I believe so."

"Is that the orphanage or the women's shelter?" the older woman wanted to know.

"I think that's the halfway house for recent drug offenders, the ones just out of jail," Rose replied.

Chariot snapped her head up at that explanation. She seemed stunned at the answer Rose gave, as if the news somehow implicated her.

"Rhonda and her beloved are forever saving the world. They're especially partial to those recently released from the big house," she said, referring to the work Rhonda and Lucas did for those just out of prison.

Rose cleared her throat, trying to get the older woman's attention. She had seen Chariot's reaction to the statement about the halfway house, but Ms. Lou Ellen hadn't seemed to notice. Rose figured she should try and change the subject.

"Of course, they did have their fair share of assistance when they got out." She waved her hands in the air as if she decided she had shared enough. "But enough about our affairs here at Shady Grove, what brings you to West Memphis, Arkansas, all the way from South Dakota?"

Rose let out a breath, relieved that her friend had gone on to another subject.

Chariot swallowed her bite and took a drink of coffee. She shook her head. "I, uh, am just traveling."

It was a shaky answer and Ms. Lou Ellen suddenly sensed that something was not quite right about the young woman sitting in the office. She studied her and then decided it was none of her business to push for any other information. She recognized a woman in trouble as easily as her daughter did. She smiled and reached over and patted Chariot on the hand.

"That's just fine," she responded. "Traveling is just fine."

Rose nodded and noticed that the guest seemed to relax a bit.

"I have never been to South Dakota," Rose said. She was standing by the counter, wiping the area around the coffeepot. "Tell me, is it still winter there?" she asked.

Chariot nodded. "It was snowing when I left," she replied.

"Snow?" Ms. Lou Ellen responded. "In April?" She seemed surprised.

"There's sometimes snow in June," Chariot added.

"Well, no wonder you are traveling. Who wants to see snow in June?" Ms. Lou Ellen folded her arms across her chest.

"I like the snow," Rose interjected. "I sort of miss it."

"You had a lot of snow in eastern North Carolina, did you?" Ms. Lou Ellen asked. Her voice carried a bit of sarcasm.

Rose finished cleaning the countertop and placed the dishrag across the edge of the sink. "No, we did not," she replied. "I mostly just miss the possibility of it."

Chariot smiled at that. "I don't think I would ever miss snow," she noted. "Or even the thought of it. I've seen enough of it to last me the rest of my life."

The other two women nodded.

"Are you traveling in search of a place that bears no mark of winter?" Ms. Lou Ellen asked.

The question seemed to confuse Chariot. She finished her biscuit and wiped her mouth off with the extra napkin the older woman placed next to her arm. "No, ma'am," she answered. "I like winter."

"Just not snow?" Rose asked. She had moved over to the table to join the two women. She sat down with a fresh cup of coffee.

"Just not snow on the plains," Chariot replied. "I'm just tired of seeing nothing but miles and miles of white. Sometimes it feels like I'm going blind."

The two women considered this observation.

"But, it's home, it's all I really know." A tear slipped from the young woman's eye and she quickly wiped it away.

"Well, it's nice to have you down south for a bit," Rose noted, trying to change the subject. She had noticed the tear.

"Do you camp?" she asked. "Would you like to stay at Shady Grove?"

Ms. Lou Ellen turned to her friend. Rose couldn't tell if she thought it was too nosy of a question.

"I have a tent," the young woman announced. "I could stay in the tent." It seemed as if the idea was one she hadn't considered. And it seemed as if she liked it.

"It's still chilly," Ms. Lou Ellen commented. Then she remembered to whom she was speaking. "But I guess a person from South Dakota can stand a little Arkansas chill."

Chariot smiled and nodded.

"You're traveling alone?" Ms. Lou Ellen asked. She glanced out the window in the direction of the car parked in front of the office.

Chariot nodded. "I left home in a hurry," she said.

"Why ever would you do that?" Ms. Lou Ellen asked. "Are you in some kind of trouble?"

There was a slight movement under the table and the older woman seemed startled to feel Rose's foot pressed against her shin. "Excuse me, Rose. Did you just kick me?" she asked, completely unaware that her friend was trying to get her attention.

"No, I'm sorry, was that your leg?" Rose asked. Then she tried to change the subject. "Do you want another biscuit?" she asked.

Chariot shook her head. "Oh, no, one was more than enough." She took another sip from her coffee. "It was very good," she added.

"It's country ham. And I add a little sugar to it. That's what makes it sweet," Ms. Lou Ellen explained.

Chariot nodded. "My grandmother used to make us ham biscuits," she said. "I haven't had one since I was a little girl."

"In South Dakota?" Ms. Lou Ellen asked.

Rose could tell that her friend was fishing for information.

There was a pause in the conversation.

"In Mitchell," Chariot replied. And then she waited. "And you're right about the other thing, too."

Ms. Lou Ellen and Rose waited for an explanation.

"I think I'm in a whole lot of trouble," she said, sounding surprised with the confession. "I think I'm in the most trouble I've ever known."

FIVE

What variety of trouble do you find yourself in?" Ms. Lou Ellen wanted to know. "Although, here at Shady Grove I doubt the brand matters much. We take all kinds, don't we, dear?" She glanced over to Rose.

Rose smiled. "I'd say we don't tend to discriminate against the troubles folks bring in."

The young woman took in a deep breath. Clearly, she wasn't sure she should elaborate about her situation to the two women. She eyed Rose and Ms. Lou Ellen. It appeared as if she was trying to read them.

"I think I'm a witness to something," she finally said.

Rose and Ms. Lou Ellen waited.

"I don't know—" She stopped. She seemed to change her mind, realizing that she wasn't ready to talk about what had happened. "Maybe I didn't see anything."

"That's fine," Ms. Lou Ellen said, recognizing the reluctance.

She patted the girl on the arm with a measure of reassurance. "You don't have to discuss your trouble. Not now, not just after your biscuit." She smiled. "But tell us, why did this trouble bring you to Arkansas?"

Chariot smiled, too, relieved not to have to explain.

"I met Rhonda at the bike rally a few years ago," she said. She could see that the two women didn't know what she meant. "In Sturgis," she added, thinking that might help make it clearer.

Neither woman responded.

"It's a big rally for motorcycle owners," she noted. "Been going on since the fifties or some time a real long time ago."

"Yes, that was ages ago," Ms. Lou Ellen said with a wink. "Before you were even a blip on your mother's radar," she added.

Chariot nodded without fully understanding the older woman. "I don't even think my mama was born until the sixties," she said.

Ms. Lou Ellen lifted her eyebrows. "I am old as dirt," she responded.

Rose laughed. "Anyway, Chariot, go on," she instructed.

"Rhonda and Lucas came to Sturgis, to the rally. It's held every year in August. And that's when I first saw them, when me and Jason met them."

Rose nodded. "When was that?" she asked.

"It was five years ago, I think." Chariot considered the question. "No, wait, it was right after Jason and I got together, right after—" She stopped. "It was four years ago. I had just moved back to Pierre," she said, obviously pulling herself together. "And I hooked up with Jason there. He was the one who had the bike," she explained. "And we went together to the rally to work at his friend's shop."

"And that's where you came in contact with my Rhonda?" Ms. Lou Ellen asked.

Chariot nodded. "She came into the store to buy a shirt."

"I bet it was black," the older woman noted.

"I, uh, don't remember," Chariot said, wondering if the older woman really thought she should know.

"I'm teasing you, child," Ms. Lou Ellen explained. "Rhonda and Lucas tend only to wear black."

Chariot smiled and nodded. "It's a biker thing," she noted.

"Yes, I guess it is." Ms. Lou Ellen placed her hands in her lap.

"They've been back to the Dakotas since then, haven't they?" Rose asked. She remembered hearing her friend talk about the big event in the summer. And she knew that the two of them had enjoyed riding around the Black Hills area. It was, she thought she recalled hearing, one of their favorite places to ride.

"It's real pretty there. And the roads are fun to drive," Chariot responded. "When there's not a lot of snow. Most bikers come back."

"It's where Rushmore is, isn't it?" Rose asked. "Near Rapid City?"

Chariot nodded. "There's lots of neat places to drive. There's the Badlands and Spearfish and there's an old western town now, too, called Deadwood." She wrapped her arms around her chest and sat back in her chair, appearing to relax a bit. "A lot of people go there to gamble," she added.

"So, you met Rhonda and Lucas at the rally," Rose noted, trying to pick the conversation back up.

"Yeah, she came in the store to buy a shirt and we started talking and we just hit it off. So later, the four of us went out to a concert and then out to Custer."

"As in the last stand?" Ms. Lou Ellen asked.

Chariot didn't understand the question.

"Custer's?" Ms. Lou Ellen added.

The young woman shrugged. She was not following the line of conversation at all.

"The general who fought the Indians and died in the battle in 1876?" Ms. Lou Ellen pulled out a handkerchief and dabbed her nose. "Never mind, dear, the incident actually occurred at Little Bighorn, which happens to be in Montana."

"I don't know," Chariot responded. "It's just the name of a little town at the state park. They let buffalo graze there and people camp and stuff."

Ms. Lou Ellen smiled. It was clear the young woman from South Dakota did not know much Indian history. She would not pursue the line of questioning any further.

"So"—Rose picked up the conversation, recognizing that Ms. Lou Ellen was not going to ask anything further about Custer and the places he had battled—"you met Rhonda and Lucas at the bike rally four years ago and now, here you are."

Chariot nodded. She knew it sounded illogical so she tried to make more sense of it. "Rhonda helped me out from time to time after we met. I used to do a lot of drugs and she was trying to help me get straight."

Ms. Lou Ellen smiled. That needed no explanation. She understood that completely.

"I finally got myself straight and I remember how she told me about her place here. She invited me and Jason to come sometime. We just"— she paused—"we never got around to it."

"I see," Rose responded.

There was a lull in the conversation.

"And so, you and Jason are no longer together and you have loaded up your belongings and decided to leave the snow and the plains and the remnants of war and bike rallies and come south." Ms. Lou Ellen smiled at herself. Clearly, she was pleased that she had figured it out. "Dear, it is quite fine that you are here and alone. I can spot man trouble from a mighty long way."

Chariot was suddenly crying.

"Now, now," Ms. Lou Ellen said as she handed the young woman her handkerchief. "We will fix you up just fine here at Shady Grove."

The young woman wiped her nose and shook her head. "No, it's not like that," she said.

"It never is," Ms. Lou Ellen said. She got up and took a glass from the cabinet. She poured Chariot a glass of water and set it in front of her. "But here's the thing, your boy may have been special and he may have been handsome riding his Harley Hog, but trust me on this one, you will find another the instant you are ready." She sat back down in her seat and touched at the sides of her hair.

"Yes, well, you should know," Rose interjected. "You have found and married enough to put you in some book of records."

Ms. Lou Ellen narrowed her glance at Rose. "Just because I have dabbled in the art of marital relations a few times—"

Rose cleared her throat. "A few times?"

"A number of times," Ms. Lou Ellen corrected herself. "That does not prohibit me from sharing my expertise with the young."

Chariot wiped her eyes and even managed a smile. "I just needed to get away," she said, without further explanation. She was trying to pull herself together.

"And this is a good place to do that," Rose said. "I should know. I did the same thing about two years ago."

Chariot looked at the woman, hoping to hear more.

"I have a little travel trailer," Rose said, seeing the curiosity on the girl's face. "Hooked it up to my Ford Bronco and headed out of North Carolina and landed in Arkansas."

"It's as if she was sent to us," Ms. Lou Ellen said, reaching over and squeezing Rose's hand.

"It's a good place to be to sort through your"—she hesitated—"through your trouble."

Chariot blushed and looked away.

"So, would you like to put your tent up or would you rather stay in one of the camping cabins we have on site?"

Rose was all business now. And she jumped up from her seat and went over to the desk to get the appropriate paperwork.

The young visitor cleared her throat and was happy to be onto another subject. "I think I'd like to stay in the tent," she replied. "I sort of like being outside now that I'm in a place where the ground is warm."

She also didn't mention, but certainly considered that being in a tent provided her with a better opportunity to be able to hear vehicles coming in case the police officer she had seen at her apartment found out where she was.

"You want to be near the river?" Rose asked, looking over the map at the available sites.

"I think I would rather be away, um, out of sight," she requested.

Ms. Lou Ellen and Rose glanced over at each other, but neither of them asked a question. It was clear that the camper was not going to reveal any more information about herself and her situation. They would leave the questions to Rhonda.

"Then we shall set you up out in one of the wooded sites," Rose said. "They're just straight down from the office, but they're the least visible." She pointed in the direction of where the most hidden tent sites were located.

Chariot nodded and immediately stood up. "I have cash," she said, reaching in her back pocket and pulling out a twenty-dollar bill. She had a small duffel bag full of cash that Jason had thrown in the backseat with the camping gear.

Rose waved it away. She knew her boss would not take her friend's money. "You and Rhonda can work that out," she said. "You'll be at number fourteen," she added.

Chariot walked over to the counter and looked on the map to find her site. She nodded. "Thank you."

"You are welcome," Rose responded. "Now, do you need some help setting up?" she asked, even though she wasn't sure she knew how to put up a tent. "I helped a group of Scouts last summer," she recalled. "I could at least hammer in a few stakes for you."

Chariot shook her head. "No, I know how to do it," she replied. She turned to Ms. Lou Ellen who was still sitting at the table. "Thank you so much for the breakfast. I'm real glad to meet you."

Ms. Lou Ellen smiled. "The pleasure is all mine and I look forward to more chats while you're here."

Chariot looked away and nodded. "I'll just go over and set up then," she announced.

"I'll let Rhonda know where you are when she arrives. Although I expect you'll hear her when she and Lucas drive up."

Chariot looked a bit confused.

"The motorcycles," Rose explained.

Then the young woman nodded. "Oh, right," and suddenly she turned pale.

"Are you okay?" Rose asked, noticing the reaction, wondering what had just caused the young woman to suddenly appear so frightened.

Chariot simply nodded and walked out the door.

The two women watched as she got into her car and drove past the office and over to the tent site.

"She's pregnant," Ms. Lou Ellen blurted out once they saw Chariot heading down the driveway.

"Now, what makes you think that?" Rose asked. She filled in the site placement in the book with a little yellow occupied tag, closed it, and set it back near the phone.

"It's obvious, dear. The tears, the mention of trouble, the sleeping on the ground." Ms. Lou Ellen had gotten up from her seat at the table and was looking out the window on the front door.

"What?" Rose asked.

"The hormones, the *trouble* . . ." Ms. Lou Ellen said, saying the last word with a lot of expression.

"No, what do you mean about sleeping on the ground? What does that have to do with being pregnant?" Rose asked.

"She wants to be closer to the earth, Mother Earth," Ms. Lou Ellen replied, as if what she was implying made perfect sense. She turned to look at her friend.

By the surprised look on her face, it was clear that Rose didn't get what the older woman was saying.

"Dear, pregnancy calls forth a woman's natural tendencies." She placed her hand over her heart.

"To sleep on the ground?" Rose asked.

"To connect with the maternal rootedness that reaches up from the soil and gives life to all things growing," Ms. Lou Ellen replied, sounding as if she was making complete sense. She turned back to the window.

Rose rolled her eyes and shook her head. "Well, I guess that explains why I never wanted to camp in a tent. I have no maternal tendencies. The only earthly rootedness I wanted to connect to was maybe a picnic on a blanket on the ground and even then I prefer a table."

"You will make a fine mother," Ms. Lou Ellen said and it was so out of the blue that it caught Rose off guard.

Ms. Lou Ellen noticed the silence and turned to see her friend staring at her. "What?" she asked.

"Why would you say that?" Rose asked.

The older woman shrugged. "Because it's true," she replied.

"Ms. Lou Ellen, I don't intend to have children," Rose said. "I'm almost forty-three years old," she added.

"Yes," her friend agreed. "At first, it startled me, too. And then Roland Harvey's wife got pregnant. She's forty-five and then I couldn't dispute what I read in the charts. My horoscope is quite clear that a baby is coming to join us at Shady Grove. It only makes sense that the message refers to you and Thomas. And I would say it's getting close to time. And when it does happen, you will see exactly what I mean about communing with the earth."

Rose shook her head. "Even if I believed your crazy astrological readings, why couldn't it just be referring to our newest camper?" she asked. "I mean if, in fact, she's pregnant."

Ms. Lou Ellen opened the door to head back to her cabin. "It clearly stated that this birth involves someone close to me. Rhonda messed herself up years ago. As far as we know, she isn't able to bear children. Mary is too old and too cranky to be a mother. And I don't have any other women that I consider close. I've worked on this thing until I have it figured it out. You are the only one. You are the chosen one. You will bring the new life to our family."

And she accentuated the end of the sentence with a strong nod of her head and left Rose standing in the midst of a prophecy that she neither welcomed nor understood.

SIX

But why would she say such a thing?" Rose wanted to know. She and Thomas were sitting side by side at a picnic table near her travel trailer. They were enjoying lunch by the river.

Thomas had walked over to the office about 11:00 A.M. and suggested that she meet him at their favorite spot. He often fixed her lunch when she worked Mary's weekday shift.

"You know how crazy she is," Thomas replied, eating his sandwich in slow, thoughtful bites. "She talked you into going shopping," he added. "I never thought I'd ever see that day."

Rose elbowed him in the side. "I shop," she said.

"Right." Tom made a face, trying to humor his girlfriend. "That's your favorite activity to do. Shopping and going to a community dance."

Rose shook her head. She had already told Thomas that she had purchased tickets for the Spring Fling. He had not been so pleased about that.

"Okay, both of those things are surprises, too. But taking me shopping to buy a dress to go dancing and telling me that I'm going to get pregnant are two completely different agendas," Rose said.

She took a bite of her sandwich. "I mean, why would she say that?" she asked, her mouth full of bread and pimento cheese.

Tom reached over and wiped her mouth. He smiled at her because he loved to watch her eat. He said that he had never seen a woman who could leave more of her food on her clothes than what she took into her stomach.

"How did it come up?" he asked.

"The new camper," Rose explained. "She guessed the girl was pregnant."

Thomas considered this clue. He had already heard about the girl that was in trouble and who had called looking for Rhonda.

"Was she reading her charts?" he asked. He knew about Ms. Lou Ellen's recent obsession with astrology. She had already found out from him the exact date, time, and place of his birth and was researching his chart.

"Yes," Rose replied.

Thomas nodded. Ms. Lou Ellen's comments were starting to make sense to him. "And correct me if I'm wrong, but didn't she say a couple of months ago that you were coming into a lot of money, based on the readings she had done?"

Rose thought about that prior prediction. She recognized what Thomas was getting at. "Yes, but later she said she had misread the part about Jupiter and that the foretelling just meant I was coming into good luck, not so much money."

"And did you, in fact, suddenly have good luck?" he pressed. He ate the last of his sandwich and folded up the plastic bag.

"Well, I guess that depends on the way you look at things," she responded. "I didn't have any bad luck," she added.

Thomas smiled. "I love Lou Ellen; don't get me wrong. But, Rose, you've been here long enough to know that she gets sort of obsessed with things. She tends to go overboard. That's why she was such a good addict."

Rose looked at Thomas. She knew that he and Ms. Lou Ellen shared a lot of history, including a recovery program. They were both alcoholics.

Thomas turned to his girlfriend and studied her. "Or is there something more to this?" he asked.

Rose waited for the rest.

"Is it that you want to get pregnant?" he asked, his voice quiet. In the midst of discussing what Ms. Lou Ellen had blurted out in a morning conversation to Rose, Thomas realized that the two of them had never really had this discussion.

He knew that Rose and her ex-husband had never felt like it was the right time to be parents, and based upon that, he had always just assumed that Rose had made up her mind about the subject. He thought she did not want to be a mother. He understood at that moment with that questioning look in her eyes, that strange expression that appeared like hope or possibility, that he may have made a false assumption.

Rose shrugged. In fairness to her boyfriend's assumption, she thought she had made that decision a while back and that it would remain unchanged. She had not wanted to have children, not with Rip, and not alone. Once in West Memphis, she had not really expected to fall in love again and she had not had time to think about the possibility of Thomas and her having a family. After all, they hadn't been together that long. And yet, somehow with her friend's crazy prediction, it seemed to bring up those considerations all over again.

A barge passed by them on the river. A low horn sounded and the splashing of the waves increased along the banks. Thomas and Rose stopped to listen. She took the last bite of her sandwich. Thomas waited for her response.

"I thought I was done thinking about motherhood. But I guess finding you, being in love, makes me think about it again," she confessed. She took the napkin and wiped off her mouth. She reached across the table and got the bag of cookies. She held it up to Thomas as an offer and he shook his head. He never cared much for sweets. He had brought the small bag of cookies for her.

"I guess it's a bigger deal than what I expected," she said. She took a bite of a cookie and breathed out a long breath.

"I always thought that turning forty really marked the end of having the opportunity to change my mind about this. I always said if I was going to get pregnant it had to happen before I turned forty. But I don't know. Lots of women my age are still having children." She leaned back, away from the table.

Thomas didn't respond. He realized in the two years' time

that they had been together it had never occurred to him that Rose might want to have children. He hadn't considered this would ever be an issue that they would discuss.

"What about you?" she asked. "You ever think about having children?"

Thomas ate a few chips and waited before answering. "Early on, I thought I did," he replied. "But I haven't thought about it for a long time. Just didn't seem the path for me."

Rose looked over at this man she loved. She slid her hand into his. "Well, maybe that was before a moon entered into your house of Saturn."

They both laughed. Neither of them knew anything about horoscopes or astrology. They usually only humored their friend when she started talking the language of the stars.

"You know, you would make a good father," she announced.

He smiled and squeezed her hand. "I think I would have done okay," he agreed.

"Done," she repeated. "As in the past tense," she added.

Thomas didn't speak for a few minutes. He could tell that this was important to Rose and he didn't want to say anything that would hurt her. He really hadn't thought about fathering a child in a long time and he surely hadn't thought about it as a part of the relationship he was in. If they came to different conclusions about the issue of parenting, he understood what they had could be over.

"I haven't seen my charts," he finally said. "But I don't really think my planet is meant to revolve in a group of little planets." He was just teasing and he knew he needed to be a bit more serious. "I don't know, Rose," he said. "I haven't thought about this in a long time. I hadn't considered starting a family at this late date in my life. I'm quite a bit older than you, remember?"

Rose nodded. Thomas was already fifty.

"Is this something you really want?" he asked.

"No." She shook her head. "I don't know," she said, changing her mind. "Ms. Lou Ellen just surprised me is all, put strange thoughts in my head. It's a question I can't answer right now."

They stopped talking when they heard the motorcycles rolling into the campground.

"They're back!" Rose announced, referring to Rhonda and Lucas. She was glad to change the subject. "And in exactly the amount of time she said it would take."

"Where were they?" Thomas wanted to know.

"Mississippi," Rose replied.

"How is it that she knew this camper from South Dakota?" he asked.

"Met her at the bike rally," Rose responded. "Rhonda said she has a history."

"What kind of history?" Thomas asked.

"A history of trouble," Rose noted. "That's all I know." She took a drink from her can of soda and then returned it to the table. "Maybe we'll know a little more now," she added.

"She's over at number fourteen, right?"

Rose nodded. "She wanted to be hidden," she recalled.

"Well, that sounds like a mystery right there," Thomas said. He pinched Rose on the arm. He knew how curious she could be about the guests at Shady Grove.

"Hey, that reminds me. That couple from Texas in the fifth wheel?"

Thomas shrugged. He didn't keep up with the campers as well as Rose and he learned most of his information from her. He rarely met anyone at the campground since he lived in a small trailer almost a half a mile away.

"There"—she pointed behind them—"that one," she noted.

Thomas turned and looked in the direction she was pointing. "Oh, okay," he replied.

"The man was in the office this morning, he's with his wife."

Thomas nodded. He waited for the rest of the story.

"They're looking for her birth family—" Rose stopped. "She was adopted," she explained.

"Okay," Thomas said.

"He was going to the courthouse to find out about the adoption laws in Arkansas, but I told him I would find out the answer to his question."

"What's the question?" Thomas asked.

"He wanted to know if the adopted person could get information about the birth parents from the adoption agency." Rose was remembering the man's question and her promise to find out the information for him. With all of the commotion around the new troubled camper from South Dakota and the odd prediction from Ms. Lou Ellen, she had forgotten what she had said that she would do.

"Don't know the answer to that one," he said. "But I'm sure that you can call social services and they could tell you," he suggested.

Rose nodded. She had already thought of that.

"Although I imagine that they don't give out that kind of information."

"Why not?" Rose asked.

"Some folks would say that it could discourage a woman from choosing adoption. If she knows that in ten or twenty years a person could come calling and come blaming her for what she did, she might decide on an abortion instead. Some folks are real touchy about private information like that."

Rose didn't respond. She thought what Thomas said made perfect sense. "What if both parties say it's okay?" she asked. She had heard of lots of adopted children finding their birth parents. The news was full of those stories.

Thomas shrugged. "I don't know," he replied. "But I figure if they've made a law against reporting the information, it would be binding in all situations."

Rose thought about the man from Texas and his wife. She guessed that even if it were possible to get the name and address of a birth parent, it would be highly unlikely that a seventy-year-old person would be able to find a parent still alive. She decided that she would call the appropriate state office that afternoon. She would still keep her promise to the man.

Both Thomas and Rose listened as the motorcycles pulled down the driveway into the campground and as the engines shut off.

"They probably stopped at Ms. Lou Ellen's," Rose commented. "She'll tell Rhonda where the girl is camped."

Thomas looked over in the direction of where the newest

camper had been assigned. "I saw her putting up her tent when I walked over to the office. I offered my help, but she seemed determined to get it done by herself."

"Yeah, I offered, too," Rose responded.

"Do you know her story?" he asked. He guessed that Rose and Ms. Lou Ellen had gotten some details about the girl. He knew that both of them could ask a lot of questions.

"She wouldn't really tell us much. She started to and then she got cold feet," Rose replied. She took off her sunglasses and cleaned them off with her shirt. "She just said that she was in trouble."

"Trouble?" Thomas asked. "What sort of trouble?"

Rose shook her head. "Didn't explain," she said.

Thomas scratched his chin thoughtfully. "And Lou Ellen figures it means she's pregnant?" he asked, recalling the earlier conversation they had.

Rose nodded.

"I suppose that's a jump you can make," he surmised.

"She did mention that she thought she had been a witness to something." Rose was remembering what had been shared by the visitor. "But when she started to elaborate, she just shut down, said that maybe she hadn't seen anything after all."

"It's odd that she would call that trouble," Thomas noted as he cleaned the space around him on the table. He placed the sandwich bag and napkins inside a larger bag.

"What do you mean?" Rose handed him her trash and he added it to the bag and then placed the bag in the picnic basket.

"I mean, if you saw something, if you were witness to something, that might put you in danger, but I don't see how that would put you in trouble."

Rose thought about his rationale. She put her sunglasses back on, drank the last from her soda, handed Thomas the can, and looked at her watch. She had left a sign on the office door that she would return in thirty minutes. She had already been away for twenty. She stood up to return to work.

Thomas stood up beside her, pulling the basket over toward him. "Trouble implies that she's done something, participated in something, but if she only saw something, I don't know why that automatically means trouble," he explained further.

"Maybe she saw something illegal and because she didn't report it, she's in trouble." Rose stretched. "Do you want to walk with me?" she asked.

He nodded. "I suppose you're right about not reporting something," Thomas agreed.

"If you witnessed something that could be classified as illegal, would you say you were in trouble?" Rose asked.

They started walking toward the office.

"I guess it depends on who else knew what I saw," he replied.

They passed a couple walking down to the river and they both smiled and waved at them.

"I bet that's it then," Rose said. "I bet somebody saw her at the thing she witnessed and now she knows that they know and, probably, they're after her. She's running scared."

Thomas reached out and took her by the hand and they continued in the direction of the office.

"Ah, if only all of life's great questions could be answered over a pimento cheese sandwich sitting on the river with the one you love," she said with a sigh.

Thomas laughed, but he knew that both of them understood that she was referring to more than just the immediate questions surrounding the latest camper to join them at Shady Grove.

SEVEN

"Well, she's not pregnant," Rhonda announced when she returned to the office. She had gone to visit with Chariot as soon as they had arrived back at Shady Grove. Lucas had stayed with his mother-in-law and then had gone over to the office when Rose returned from lunch.

Lucas, Ms. Lou Ellen, and Rose were sitting at the table trying to figure out a sudoku puzzle that had been in a newspaper that was placed in the campground's recycling bin located next to the office sometime earlier that day. Rose had taken out a stack of papers to search for puzzles before leaving for lunch.

Sudoku had become the latest form of entertainment for the management team at Shady Grove and they always searched for puzzles in any of the newspapers that campers brought with them into Shady Grove. Lucas and Ms. Lou Ellen were particularly big fans of the number puzzles.

Thomas had left them a bit earlier to go into town to buy

groceries. He was planning to cook for Rose later in the evening. She had requested pot roast and new potatoes. Ms. Lou Ellen had teased Thomas for spoiling his girlfriend and had also made sure to give a passing comment about marriage and growing a family. Both Thomas and Rose had pretended not to hear.

Rhonda closed the door behind her and stood by the counter. She leaned her hip against the door, pulled her hair out of the ponytail it had been in, and then swept it back up, combing the loose hairs with her fingers. She gave a sigh.

"So, let's not plan a baby shower just yet, shall we?" She was speaking to her mother, who simply waved away the comment.

"So, what's her trouble?" Rose asked. She slid the paper closer to Lucas. Unlike the other two at the table, she could never seem to grasp how to solve the number puzzles. She was a crossword person herself, preferring word answers since she never considered herself to be very good with any kind of math equation.

"She left Pierre in a hurry," Rhonda replied. She went around the counter and sat down at the desk. "She said she saw something," she added.

Rose got up and went over to where Rhonda was sitting. She sat down in the chair across from the desk. She folded her arms across her chest and slumped down, waiting for more of the story.

"That's old news," Ms. Lou Ellen stated. "She already confessed to that." She paused. "Son, you can't use an eight, there's already the number eight on that line," she said to Lucas. She was pointing to a line in the puzzle.

"Well, Mother dear, I can't pay attention to what numbers have been used if you keep moving the puzzle away from me." Lucas was a portrait of patience. "Why don't you finish this one and I'll do the one in the magazine?" he asked.

He reached over and got a local magazine that always featured a sudoku puzzle in the back. He opened it and folded back the pages and started working. His reading glasses fell down the bridge of his nose.

"Well," Rose waited, paying no attention to what was going on at the table behind her. "What did she see?"

There was a deliberate pause.

"A murder," Rhonda finally replied. "Early Monday morning."

The three others in the room all snapped up their heads and turned in her direction.

"Murder?" Ms. Lou Ellen asked, shaking her head. "And having a baby?" she added. Then she looked down again to study her puzzle. "It's a six!" she shouted and clapped her hands together.

"Mother, there is no baby," Rhonda said again. "Why do you have that in your mind?" she asked.

Rose turned around to get a closer look at the older woman and to discourage her from telling Rhonda and Lucas about what she had shared with her. Ms. Lou Ellen was already staring in her direction.

"I don't know," Ms. Lou Ellen responded. "Must be in the stars," she added and then winked at Rose.

Rose blushed and turned to make sure that neither Rhonda nor Lucas had noticed. They didn't let on if they had sensed anything more to what Ms. Lou Ellen was implying.

"Whose murder?" Rose asked, glad to get back to the main story of interest.

"Should we go over to pray with her?" Lucas asked before his wife could answer the question. He had closed the magazine and taken off his reading glasses. He turned to face his wife.

Rhonda shook her head. "Not right now, I think," she replied. "Maybe later in the afternoon." She seemed reluctant to share the rest of her news. She watched her husband.

Lucas nodded and turned back so that he was once again sitting with his legs under the table. He bowed his head and the women could see that he was praying. Accustomed to his silent prayers, they carried on their conversation quietly.

"It was . . ." Rhonda was going to answer Rose, but she waited until her husband had finished his prayer. "Lucas, it was Jason."

The man looked up at his wife. It wasn't the news he expected to hear. He shook his head and then bowed again in what appeared to be another prayer.

"It was sometime in the middle of the night and they were packing to leave South Dakota. She had taken a load of stuff to the car and she said that she put the belongings in the backseat and started the engine to warm it up. She cleaned off the windshield and when she got back to the apartment she discovered that he had been shot."

"She didn't see who did it?" Rose asked.

Rhonda shook her head. "She saw a man leave and she said that he had also followed her part of the way here," she replied.

"Why didn't she call the police?" Rose was curious about

why the girl would run instead of seeking help in the town or at least in the state where the murder occurred.

Rhonda shrugged. "She wouldn't say. She just said that she didn't know who to trust and that she didn't have anyone else to contact."

"Amen," Lucas said, ending his quiet meditation. "Jason is dead?" he asked. The news had really shaken him.

Rhonda nodded solemnly. "I'm afraid so," she replied.

The room grew silent as Rhonda and Lucas thought about the man who had been killed, the young boy they had gotten to know from South Dakota.

"He was a good kid," Lucas said. He folded his hands in front of him.

The women assumed he was going to pray again, but he just looked ahead.

"Chariot said you met each other at a bike rally?" Rose asked. She recalled what had already been said about their friendship.

Rhonda nodded. "We rode around with them that year and then went back again to see some other parts of the area."

"We tried to help them a bit," Lucas added. "They had both struggled with drugs and were messed up most of the time."

"I think she had done a little jail time," Rhonda said. "And was having a hard time being out."

"Rhonda was like a big sister to her that first time we met," Lucas said.

The two of them smiled at each other. He was proud of the way his wife cared for others who had walked a path similar to her own.

"She just needed a little guidance," Rhonda said.

"Sounds like she still needs it," Ms. Lou Ellen noted.

Lucas nodded.

"What do you know about him, the boyfriend?" Rose asked.

Rhonda shook her head. "Not much," she replied. "We were really only around the two of them a couple of times," she added. "Unlike Chariot, he seemed to have a good head on his shoulders."

"She's just young, love," Lucas said, referring to the woman who was sitting in her tent at the edge of the woods while they discussed her a few hundred yards away. "She does okay for where she's come from," he explained.

Ms. Lou Ellen lifted her head and studied her son-in-law. "What does she come from?" she asked. She placed the pen down on the paper in front of her. "No, wait, let me guess."

The three waited for her to finish.

"Trouble," she answered her own question.

Rhonda smiled at her mother. She nodded.

"If I remember the story correctly," Lucas spoke quietly and with thoughtful consideration. "Her father is dead after being shot by her mother. She was cleared of the charges because she said it was self-defense and that he had almost killed her before she was able to shoot him. As a result, her mother has been in a wheelchair and incapacitated for most of young Chariot's life. I also think the woman is prone to drink now and again."

"I get that," Ms. Lou Ellen responded.

Lucas reached over and patted his mother-in-law on the arm. "But you have been delivered," he announced with a big smile on his face. "We've all been," he added, "and now we must pray for those who are not." He pulled his hand away and bowed his head again.

The three women waited this time before continuing their conversation. Ms. Lou Ellen and Rhonda bowed their heads and closed their eyes. Rose just watched. She was used to how the Boyd family included prayer as a part of their table talk as if God was simply another person sitting around the table. She respected their faith, but she didn't always join them in the physical ways that they engaged in prayer. She didn't usually bow or close her eyes. She just held the last thought of the person mentioned in a cloud of light. She waited until Lucas signaled the end of the silent prayer.

"Amen," he said and Rhonda and her mother glanced up. The conversation continued as if there had been no divine disruption.

"Jason said Chariot and her mother never really got along," Rhonda explained. She pushed herself away from the desk and stretched out her legs. She crossed her feet at the ankles.

"He said that Chariot lived with her grandmother most of her childhood while her mother stayed with Chariot's sister next door. No one really talks about why Chariot left home and why she didn't stay with her mother."

"I never understood why Jason and Chariot stayed in South Dakota," Lucas remarked. "Neither one of them seemed all that crazy about living there."

"You would think with a family history like she had that she would have wanted to leave," Rhonda speculated.

"Oh, I don't know," Rose responded. "Even with crazy families, loyalty is still an issue." She hesitated. "Believe me, I know," she added. "Home is with the folks who know you best, even if they're nuttier than fruitcakes."

"Yes, but you did eventually leave," Rhonda said.

They all knew about Rose's family history, her father's alcoholism and her childhood abuse.

"Not for a very long time," Rose explained. "I was almost twice Chariot's age before I packed up my little Casita and drove away."

"But you did it," Ms. Lou Ellen said with a nod in Rose's direction. "And you are still a young enough woman," she added.

Rose sat up in her chair.

"Young enough for what, Mother dear?" Lucas wanted to know.

The room fell silent. Rose really didn't want her employers and friends to know what Ms. Lou Ellen had predicted for her. She just wasn't ready to talk about motherhood with a group of people.

"Young enough to enjoy life," Ms. Lou Ellen replied. She shrugged as if it was a completely innocent notion.

"That's a true statement, Mother," Lucas said.

"Well, back to Chariot, I think there was something holding her in Pierre, something she would never talk about," Rhonda said. "But it was real and it kept her there even when Jason tried to find work in Minneapolis."

"She sounded to me like she was eager to get out of South Dakota," Ms. Lou Ellen recalled, remembering the conversation she had with Chariot when she first arrived. "She said she was tired of snow."

"I still don't understand why she wouldn't call the police when she found her boyfriend's body, when she saw the man who she assumed had done it," Rose said. "And how did she know that he was really dead?" she asked.

Even trained as a nurse, Rose hadn't always been able to tell when a person was dead. Sometimes a person appeared to have died, but there was still a pulse, still breath in the body that could only be determined with a stethoscope or some other medical equipment. She knew that an untrained person couldn't possibly know for certain whether or not a man was dead or just seriously injured.

"Shouldn't she have at least called an ambulance?" Rose shook her head. Things weren't making a lot of sense to her.

"Jason told her to leave," Rhonda explained. "He wasn't dead when she found him. He had been shot, but was still conscious, and he told her that she was in danger and that she needed to leave."

"So, the boyfriend might not be dead?" Ms. Lou Ellen asked.

"No," Rhonda replied. "She was pretty sure that he died right after that."

"Then what happened?" Rose wanted to know.

"Then she got in her car and drove to Arkansas," Rhonda replied.

Lucas began tapping his pencil on the table. He was clearly thinking about the situation. "I don't know, sisters," he said.

"I don't mean to doubt our young friend, but something just doesn't seem quite right about this," he noted.

"I have to agree with Lucas." Ms. Lou Ellen spoke to her daughter. "She's not telling you everything."

"Like what else?" Rhonda asked.

"Like why were they leaving in the middle of the night to begin with? And why didn't she call 911 to send an ambulance even though she had left?" Rose was listing a number of the things that bothered her. It just didn't seem to her that the young woman from South Dakota was being completely honest about what happened in Pierre, what happened to Jason.

"And why is there a report of the police looking for a woman by the name of Chariot Stevens who is suspected of killing her boyfriend, Jason Holmes?" Ms. Lou Ellen had started reading the newspaper that carried the puzzle she was working and found the story right on the front page.

EIGHT

The phone rang before any of the others could react to Ms. Lou Ellen's discovery from the newspaper on the table. Rose reached across the desk in Rhonda's direction and answered it.

"Shady Grove," she said.

"Why you not answer like I taught you?"

Rose smiled. She knew immediately from the broken English and the hint of sarcasm that the caller was Mary, the manager of Shady Grove and the friend of everyone gathered in the office. "Because I knew it was you and I just wanted to get your goat."

"Why you think I got a goat?" she asked, not understanding the metaphor.

"Never mind," Rose replied.

Rhonda got up and walked over to the table to read the article in the paper that Ms. Lou Ellen and Lucas were hunched over.

Rose tried to hear anything that they were saying, but she couldn't make out any words. She leaned closer to the group.

"Are you enjoying being in Little Rock with your sister?" Rose asked, trying to sound interested in Mary's call. She knew that the woman from overseas had never visited Mary and that Mary had made lots of plans for the two of them while she was in town. It had been the first time she had ever taken time away from the campground. There were also some other friends of the family in that part of the state so they were spending a lot of time reuniting with old relations.

"We eat so much I have to buy new pants," Mary replied. "Phong never have French fries or Big Whopper or chocolate syrup. All we do is eat," she added.

Rose laughed. "Well, I don't know about your sister, but you could use a few extra pounds anyway. You're kind of skinny with a mouth that's too big. You need to gain some weight so that your voice isn't so much larger than your body."

"I not so loud," Mary argued. "You should hear my sister. Listen."

Rose could tell that her friend had held out the receiver so that Rose could hear the conversation going on around her. Mary was right; there was one very loud and distinctive voice that sounded familiar. She guessed that this was her sister talking in the background.

"Is Phong older or younger than you?" Rose asked. She had not remembered what Mary had told them about the visiting sibling.

"She a twin," came the answer.

"Your twin?" Rose asked. "I didn't know you had a twin," she said. "Is she identical to you?"

"We look exactly the same, only she used to be fatter. But not anymore," she noted.

"I know, Big Whopper and chocolate syrup."

The two of them laughed.

"So, what is going on at Shady Grove?" Mary asked. "You close office since I'm gone?"

"Can't you enjoy your vacation without worrying about us?" Rose asked. She had known that her manager would call. In fact, she was surprised that Mary had waited a couple of days before checking in with her. Mary had worked at least two weeks trying to make sure that Rose knew everything about running the Shady Grove office before she would even agree to take the time away.

"I figure you mess everything up for me so that I have to work extra when I get back," she explained. "I call now to see if I can fix it."

"Well, I am happy to report that I haven't broken anything for three entire days. Of course, that is mostly because we have had only a couple of guests check in since you left." Rose knew that Mary loved to think of herself as the most competent of the Shady Grove staff. Rose thought she would feed the manager's ego a bit.

"You take any reservations?" Mary asked.

"A few for early summer," Rose replied. "Nothing too complicated though. I left you all the work of charging their credit cards and confirming them."

"You clean out toilets and take out trash from laundry room?"

"Will you leave me alone?" Rose said. "I know what I'm doing here. You just stay in Little Rock and eat. Worry your sister."

"Pssst." It was the sound Mary liked to make when she became impatient. "She worry me."

Rose laughed. "Good," she replied. "You need somebody to let you know how annoying you can be."

"Ah, you miss me," Mary said.

"More than you'll ever know," Rose said. "You want to talk to Rhonda?" she asked.

Rhonda glanced up from the table where she had been reading the paper and walked over to the desk and took the receiver. Rose headed over to take her spot and to catch up on the story that the others had read and that she had missed.

"What's it say?" she asked.

Since she was finished, Ms. Lou Ellen slid the paper over to where Rose could read it. Lucas was shaking his head and making a kind of clucking noise as if he were worried or disappointed, Rose couldn't tell which. She started to read.

The article in the *Tribune* didn't reveal too much information. It only noted that a body had been found at an apartment complex near downtown Pierre and that it had been identified as Jason Humphrey Holmes. It read that there had been a report of gunfire in the area and that when the police arrived they had found the victim, shot and lying in the hallway of his apartment.

The police were most interested in locating the other apartment tenant, the victim's girlfriend, a woman known as Chariot

Stevens. It cited two eyewitnesses. There was one who reported that he had seen the woman fleeing the vicinity and the other, a next-door neighbor, who claimed he had seen her shoot the victim.

Rose finished reading the article and scanned the rest of the front-page news for more information, but found only the anchor story about a senator's daughter, a beautiful young woman from Mitchell, who had just won a beauty contest and a big scholarship. There was a large photograph accompanying the story. Below that one was also a small article about the senator from Mitchell and her history in targeting drug dealers in the state. There was also something about how she was planning to turn over much of her work against drugs to someone else because she was considering a run for national office. There was nothing else about the murder. She looked up to see Lucas bowed in prayer and Ms. Lou Ellen shaking her head.

Rhonda was finishing her conversation with Mary.

"Well, just make sure you bring her by here before she leaves to go back to Vietnam. It would be awful if we didn't get a chance to meet her."

Then there were a few other greetings exchanged and Rhonda hung up the phone. "They're visiting family and mostly just eating," she said to the others, summing up her phone conversation.

Rose smiled. "She said she had to buy new clothes she had gained so much weight."

"I wish I would have known," Ms. Lou Ellen responded. "I would love to help Mary pick out some new things for spring."

"Yes, I hear you're taking the staff shopping," Rhonda said, referring to Lou Ellen's plan to buy Rose a new dress.

"Yes, dear, it is true, but if you are perturbed or jealous even in the slightest way, you know that you are welcome to join the two of us. I'd love nothing more than to purchase a lovely spring frock for you." She winked at Rhonda.

"Never mind," Rhonda said, wanting to turn the conversation back to what they had all just read. "What does everyone think about the story?" she asked. She noticed her husband in a prayerful position. She looked at the other two.

"Sounds pretty incriminating," Rose replied.

"It seems odd that they would be allowed to report eyewitness accounts," Ms. Lou Ellen said. "I thought that they tried to keep that kind of thing quiet to use in the trial. I thought such information could prejudice a jury and therefore create difficulties for the prosecution."

"Maybe there was just a guy eager for his fifteen minutes of fame, someone the reporter got to before the police did," Rose guessed, shrugging.

"What's the date on that paper?" Rhonda wanted to know.

Rose scanned the top of the page. "It's from a couple of days ago," she said. "And it has to be from Chariot, she's the only South Dakota person here at Shady Grove."

"She just got here this morning, right?" Rhonda asked.

Rose nodded. "She must have gotten the paper before she left."

The women heard Lucas mutter a quiet amen and then rejoin their discussion.

"So, she stayed in the area after it happened?" Rhonda asked

"It appears so, dear," Ms. Lou Ellen replied.

"But why would she wait around to get a paper before leaving?" Lucas was the one to ask what they were all wondering. After his prayer, he was fully engaged in trying to understand what was happening with the young woman he considered to be a friend.

"And where in the area was she waiting around?" Rose asked.

"It doesn't make any sense," Rhonda noted.

"Well, let's think about this." Lucas leaned back in his chair. He threw his hands behind his head.

The women listened.

"If I remember right, it's about eight hundred miles from Pierre to West Memphis. Doesn't that seem right, Rhon?" he asked.

His wife nodded.

"It took us a couple of days to make the trip, but we were on the bikes," he recalled. "In a car, however, a person could drive that far in about twelve or thirteen hours."

The women waited for him to continue.

"If the murder happened early in the morning on Monday, and she left town right after it occurred. . . ." He sat forward in his chair again and rested his elbows on the table in front of him. He was thinking about his theory. "Then she was hiding somewhere all day Monday and Monday night before getting a Huron newspaper on Tuesday morning."

The three others nodded, following the chronological series of events.

"Then she drove like a released bat out of hell on Tuesday to arrive in Memphis sometime during the morning of today," Ms. Lou Ellen finished her son-in-law's description of the proposed time frame.

"So, where was she all day Monday?" Rose asked.

"She mentioned that she was from Mitchell," Ms. Lou Ellen noted, recalling the conversation they had when the young woman first arrived.

"Where's that?" Rose asked.

Rhonda walked over to the counter and pulled out an atlas from behind it, opening it to South Dakota. She glanced across the state until she found the town of Mitchell, and then she measured the distance to Huron using the small scale included at the top of the page. "It's about forty miles south of Huron," she said.

"So, she visited her crazy family before making a run for it," Ms. Lou Ellen guessed.

Lucas, Rhonda, and Rose were quiet, carefully considering everything they had discussed.

"I guess she was staying with family members and then saw the article in the paper and knew she had to get out of town quick." Rose shared her theory.

"Or maybe she met with her crazy mama and got some tips on how to cover up a murder." Ms. Lou Ellen was obviously going with a very different theory, incorporating the part of Chariot's family history that Lucas had shared.

"Or maybe it's just none of our business what she was doing before she got to us and we just treat her as a sister in trouble." Rhonda closed the atlas and glanced over at the others. "Maybe she just needed to be with family a little while before running away and we don't need to know any more details." She had obviously grown tired of all the speculation and talk in which the four of them had been engaged.

Lucas smiled. He winked at Rhonda. "That is exactly what it is, none of our business, and I seek forgiveness for messing in details that I don't need to know."

Ms. Lou Ellen narrowed her glance toward her son-in-law. "Oh, Lucas," she said, waving her hand in a dismissive action. "Just because we like to figure out details doesn't mean we will judge."

Lucas gave his mother-in-law a look of skepticism.

"Maybe we need to sort through the details because we're the ones who are going to have to help her figure all of this mess out," Rose noted. She was not ready to give up on solving the mystery of their newest guest at Shady Grove.

"What is this name anyway?" Ms. Lou Ellen asked. "I've never met anybody by the name of Chariot."

"Yeah, that is odd," Rose agreed.

Rhonda smiled. She and Lucas exchanged a knowing look. "We asked that, too, the first time we met her," she said.

"It seems like her mother had taken to Scripture reading during her pregnancy. She went into labor just after she finished reading the Bible story in Kings Two about the passing of the prophet Elijah, the story that was the inspiration for the old song, 'Swing Low, Sweet Chariot.' It's about the band of angels coming after Elijah, taking him on from this world to the next," Lucas recalled.

"Anyway, Chariot's mother told her daughter that the labor and delivery hurt so much she thought the chariots of fire from heaven had come down and were taking her on to her home in glory. She said she thought for sure she was dying. When her pain had eased enough to finally answer the question regarding the name of the baby, she told them Chariot." Rhonda finished the story for her husband.

There was a pause.

"So, she named her child after what she thought had killed her?" Rose asked for clarification.

"I suppose that's one way of looking at it," Lucas replied.

"Well, I guess it could be a lot worse," Ms. Lou Ellen noted, fanning herself with the folded newspaper she had in her hand. "Her mother could have been reading the story of Noah."

The others waited.

"Then the child would have been called Flood or High Water."

"Or how about what killed Lot's wife?" Rose asked, going along with her friend.

"Salt," they both said at the same time. They snickered at each other while Lucas and Rhonda just watched.

"Sisters." Lucas was just about to scold the two of them for being disrespectful when they all heard a car drive up.

It was Rose who walked over to the door and looked out the window to see who was arriving at Shady Grove. She was laughing until she glanced out and recognized the vehicle. She turned around somberly to announce it to the others.

"It's the sheriff," was all she said. And everything about the mood of the room suddenly changed.

NINE

"Good afternoon, everyone," Sheriff Montgomery said as he walked in the door. He was carrying his hat under his arm and was holding a clipboard in his hand. He had lost some weight over the winter season and he looked fit and youthful.

"Sheriff," Rose said as a means of greeting. She had walked around the counter and was standing awkwardly at the desk.

Lucas stood to shake the man's hand while Rhonda stayed at the counter and waved in his direction. She was leaning on her elbows. Sheriff Montgomery put down his clipboard on the counter to receive Lucas's greeting. The two smiled at each other.

"Hello, Leon," Ms. Lou Ellen said. She slid the South Dakota paper toward herself on the table and then placed her arms over it as inconspicuously as she could.

"Lou Ellen." He nodded at the older woman.

"What brings you out here?" Rose asked, and then wondered if her voice sounded as nervous as she felt.

"Can't a friend stop to visit?" Sheriff Montgomery asked with a smile. He glanced around at the others in the room. He seemed to notice the awkwardness in the group.

"Of course, of course," Lucas replied. He let go of the sheriff's hand and gestured for him to go over to the table and sit.

The sheriff went over and sat down across from Ms. Lou Ellen. Lucas remained over near the counter with Rhonda while Rose stayed leaning against the desk.

"It's quite a lovely day today," Ms. Lou Ellen offered as a way to open up the conversation. She was pressing her upper body forward with the paper securely under her arms on the table.

"Yes, ma'am," Montgomery responded. "I think maybe we're going to get our spring after all," he added.

Everyone nodded.

"Ya'll just get back from a trip?" he asked of Lucas.

Lucas nodded. "We were down in Mississippi," he replied. "We go to a little spot there every few months. Rhonda likes to visit friends."

The sheriff nodded and smiled. He knew all about the good work that the Boyds did along the river. He had been with them on a few of their mission activities. The three of them had been a part of rebuilding some houses on the Gulf Coast after Katrina as well as getting supplies to a town in Oklahoma after a series of deadly tornadoes. He looked around again at the foursome in the office, still feeling the tension in the room.

"Did I interrupt something?" he asked.

They all spoke up at the same time, "Oh, no!" they said, a bit too enthusiastically.

Rose immediately sat down at the desk and started shuffling papers, trying to appear as if she had work to do.

"We were just speaking of campground things," Lucas responded. "Necessary repairs, maintenance issues, that kind of thing."

Rhonda cleared her throat and went to stand behind Rose. "Do I need to help look over the reservations?" she asked.

"No, no," Rose replied. "That's all taken care of." She moved a pile of papers from one side of the desk to the other.

There was an awkward pause.

"You have anybody interesting come to camp with you this week?" the sheriff asked.

The four others in the office suddenly began looking at one another, waiting for someone to answer the question. There were coughs and immediate shifts in body language. The sheriff just watched them.

"There's a lovely couple from Texas," Rose said quickly. "They have a fifth wheel, parked by the river." She tried to think of something else to add. "They've gone to look for the woman's birth parents, somewhere near the border of Missouri."

Montgomery nodded. He continued to search the faces around the room, trying to understand if something was wrong at Shady Grove.

"By the way, Sheriff," Rose asked, thinking it would be a great means of diverting attention from bringing up any other identities of campers, "can you get the name of birth parents in Arkansas?"

"I don't know what you mean," he replied.

It had worked. He had quit looking around the room and was involved in her line of questioning.

"I mean, if an adopted person from here wanted to find out the name of her birth mother, would the state or the adoption agency give it to them?" she asked. She was proud of herself for moving the conversation into a different direction.

The sheriff considered the question. "I can't say as if I really know the answer to that," he said. Then he scratched his chin and sat back in his seat. "I would have to ask somebody over at the courthouse," he added.

Rose nodded. "I know in North Carolina that adoption agencies or the department of social services can't tell," she said. "I remember that from the hospital," she explained. "Thomas said it was to protect the women who give up their children." She was trying hard to make small talk.

"That makes sense," the sheriff agreed. "I never met anybody trying to find their birth parents," he noted. "I'm not sure how one goes about that process."

"I heard somebody say there was a Web site where you could pay a couple of thousand dollars and that within twenty-four hours they can give you a name and an address," Rhonda said. She was glad for Rose's topic of conversation.

"That Internet is amazing," Lucas commented.

"It's just lovely to be able to find out about people, isn't it?" Ms. Lou Ellen jumped in.

"You can type in a name and get the latest information on anybody," Rose chimed in. "You can Google a person and find out if there have been any stories about them in the newspapers or magazines."

And as soon as the words left her mouth, Rose felt her throat go dry. The others watched as her face grew pale. In a knee-jerk reaction, Ms. Lou Ellen slid the newspaper she was hiding with her elbow and it immediately fell on the floor around her. The different sections scattered around her feet.

Sheriff Montgomery stood from his seat and bent down to help pick up the sections. Lucas ran over and bumped him, almost causing him to fall. Lucas was, after all, a big man. "No, no!" he exclaimed. "I'll get that!"

Sheriff Montgomery eyed the group. Rhonda and Lucas were yanking up the pages while Ms. Lou Ellen just sat fanning herself with a handkerchief. Rose had stood up at the desk and had a frantic look on her face.

"What is wrong with you people?" he asked.

They all froze as if they had been caught at doing something illegal.

It was Lucas to answer. "Brother Leon," he said as he handed his wife the newspaper. She took it and walked over to the counter. Lucas reached over and patted the sheriff on the arm. "We have just heard some sad news about a friend of ours," he explained.

The women watched closely.

"There's been a death," he added, "and we were just trying to understand what we should do for the family in this difficult time." He shook his head.

Sheriff Montgomery surveyed the group of friends and they all responded with nods or sympathetic responses.

"Well, who is it?" he asked. His voice still sounded a bit suspicious.

"It's a young boy," Ms. Lou Ellen answered for the group. "He's not from here," she explained. "And he had just discovered he was going to be a father." She dabbed at her eyes with her handkerchief.

Rose and Rhonda looked at each other, rolling their eyes.

The sheriff didn't notice the exchange. He sat back down. "Well, that's too bad," he replied. "Too bad for everybody."

The group settled as there seemed to be a collective silent sigh of relief.

"Well," the sheriff said, looking to change the subject and get to the purpose of his appearance. He was growing tired of the strange visit with the staff of Shady Grove. "The reason I'm here is because I would like to get a few tickets to the Spring Fling," he explained. "I ran into Thomas in town and he mentioned that you still have some." He was speaking to Ms. Lou Ellen.

"I do, it's true," she replied. "Although I have sold almost all of mine," she mentioned. She winked at Rose. "I'm even taking one attendee shopping next week. Maybe we could purchase you a new tie."

Sheriff Montgomery didn't respond. He instead turned to Rose. "You and Thomas going?" he asked.

Rose nodded without much hesitation. "It appears as if I have been recruited," she replied.

"Well, that's nice," Montgomery noted. "It's a good event for the community," he added.

"How many tickets will you be needing?" Ms. Lou Ellen asked, thinking he was purchasing them for staff in his department.

"Two," he replied.

"Two?" she repeated. "Are these for you and a special someone?" she asked. She lifted her eyebrows and waited for his response.

He cleared his throat, suddenly realizing that he was the one displaying a certain level of discomfort.

"I knew you were spiffying yourself up for a woman," she added. She clapped her hands together. "All that weight you've lost, a new hairstyle . . ." She crossed her arms at the wrists and placed them across her heart.

"It's Loretta Cleaver, isn't it?" Ms. Lou Ellen was delighted with the thought that she had figured out a new couple in town.

"Mother, I don't really think you should be so curious," Rhonda said.

Suddenly Ms. Lou Ellen leaned across the table toward the officer. "Do you have on cologne, Sheriff?" she asked.

The question flustered the sheriff and he made a kind of coughing noise. His face reddened. "No, no," he replied. "Probably just the laundry detergent I used," he said.

The others smiled. Suddenly, the tables were turned and Rose and Rhonda and Lucas were relieved. Besides, they loved watching the older woman work.

"No, I'm pretty sure that's cologne," Ms. Lou Ellen noted, sitting up and moving closer to try and smell him. "I believe that's Mr. Calvin Klein's brand." She smiled. "I think one of my husbands used to wear it. What is it, Obsession or Possession or Recession? I don't recall."

She waved her hand at her daughter. "Come over here, Rhonda, smell the sheriff. Now, was it Mr. Maddox who wore that or Lester Earl?" she asked.

Rhonda stepped over to the table, going along with her mother. She stuck her face by the sheriff's neck. "I don't remember that particular smell," she said. "Must have been one of the husbands I didn't get the privilege of sniffing."

"I think it may have been one of the later ones."

Both women were leaning into the sheriff.

"Let me smell," came from the other side of the room, and Rose joined them.

"What are you doing?" Sheriff Montgomery jumped from his chair. His face was crimson. "I said it was just the detergent." He tried to compose himself. He adjusted his tie and pulled on the waistband of his pants. He picked up his hat and placed it squarely on his head. He was standing near the wall as far away from the three women as he could get.

Lucas grinned at the scene taking place before him. "You can't get anything over on these three, Leon."

"Well, I'm not trying to get anything over," the man replied. "Look, if you don't have the tickets, I'll just get them from Martha Foote. I know she has some over at the diner." He kept his distance.

"Oh, Leon," Ms. Lou Ellen said as she rose from her seat. "Don't be so sensitive." She waved her hands in front of her face. "The tickets are at my place. I'll go get them." She headed toward the door and then turned around. "It really is no concern to us if you decided to put on a little aftershave or if you have a new lady friend. For heaven's sake, it's nice." She added, "Actually, it's kind of sexy, Sheriff." And she winked and walked out.

The sheriff shifted his weight from side to side. He slid his hand over his chin and then readjusted his hat.

"Mother does have a way, doesn't she?" Rhonda smiled.

Montgomery was still standing a bit away from the two women. They noticed his stance and walked to the desk, giving him back his personal space, which seemed to calm him.

"Are you here for a while?" Montgomery asked Lucas.

Lucas nodded. "I think I'm going to work a little on the sites near the woods," he replied. "I've been having a little trouble with the outlets over there."

"Oh," the sheriff noted. "You want me to take a look?" he asked. "I'd like to put those courses in electrical wiring we took at the community college to good use."

Rose and Rhonda shouted in unison, *"No!"* They knew that Chariot was camped at one of the sites that needed fixing.

Sheriff Montgomery turned in their direction.

"This is something Lucas needs to figure out for himself." Rhonda recovered as quickly as possible. "He needs to work on the wiring more than you," she added.

"That's real fine of you, Leon," Lucas said, taking his wife's lead. "But Rhonda's right. I took those classes to be able to take care of some of these projects around here and I need to practice on my own."

Montgomery nodded. "All right," he responded. "I'll just save my newfound skills for the next housing project we do on the Gulf Coast."

The three others nodded.

"Why don't I walk you over to Mother's cabin?" Rhonda asked. She had decided that this visit had gone on long enough. "I was going out and if we meet her outside that would save her a few extra steps," she explained.

Sheriff Montgomery turned to her and nodded. "Okay," he agreed.

The two of them moved toward the door. He picked up the clipboard he had left on the counter.

"We'll see you, Rose," he said.

"Yes, Sheriff, glad you stopped by," she said with a smile that seemed a little too big to the officer.

Rhonda opened the door and the sheriff suddenly turned back around to face the three of them.

"By the way," he said. "Jimmy Novack mentioned that a woman driving a car with South Dakota license plates was looking for your place. He said she acted real strange, jumpy, nervous-like."

Rose looked at Rhonda. Her eyes were as big as saucers.

"Seems I need to find her," he continued. "Jimmy has a surveillance camera so I can get the number of the plate from that and have a go at trying to locate her. But I just figured I'd ask you if she was here before I went to all that work." He paused, watching the reaction of the three in the office. "You all know anything about her?"

It was a good few minutes before anyone could answer.

TEN

It turned out that Chariot had taken out her purse while she pumped her gas and then left it on the trunk of the car. When she took off, she had forgotten where she had placed it, and even though she had kept her wallet with her, her pocketbook had gone flying in the air when she exited. Jimmy was trying to locate her to return the missing piece of property.

Rose, calm and deliberate, told the sheriff that the girl had stopped by, but that she had left for the afternoon. She informed him that she or Rhonda would go by the station and pick up the purse to give to the girl if she came back or if she was gone, Rose had lied, someone would make sure it was mailed to her home in South Dakota.

Sheriff Montgomery appeared to have bought the solution and that was the end of the conversation. He left the office with Rhonda and picked up his tickets from Ms. Lou Ellen and departed Shady Grove. They all watched him leave, driving out past the campers, past the tents. Rose hoped he didn't see Chariot's campsite.

Rhonda and Lucas went to their trailer to take care of some errands and to let Chariot know about her purse at Jimmy's service station. Rose finished her work for the day.

She closed the office late in the afternoon, booking two more sites and answering a lot of questions from campers before she taped a credit card receipt and site directions on the door for the man who had called and made a reservation, but had said that he wouldn't arrive until after-hours.

Before she left the office, a family from Michigan was traveling south and wanted a corner site near the river since they were planning to stay a few days, and a couple from Georgia was heading west, just stopping over to rest before getting up early to try and make it to Amarillo, Texas, by evening the next day. They didn't care where they parked, just as long as it was quiet and easy to pull out of in the morning. Rose took care of the campers and assisted them in finding their sites.

She left in the golf cart and headed over from the office to clean the showers and laundry room; she was late with her errands, way past the designated time for that task. When Mary was working, the facilities were cleaned every day from 1:00 to 2:00 P.M. The signs on the buildings noted the times they were closed. There was never alteration to that schedule. Once Rose started filling in, she often didn't get to them in the specified time. She frequently found herself running behind schedule because she spent too much time talking to folks, hearing their stories, helping them settle in. She hoped no one would complain about the late hour of the maintenance.

She checked the laundry room first, cleaning out the filters in the dryers, straightening up the magazine rack, placing the chairs under the table, dusting off the shelves, and putting the hangers back on the drying rod. She collected the trash and vacuumed, wiped off the appliances, and finally turned off the light. And then she went behind the building to work on the restrooms and showers.

She went in the men's room first, propped open the door with the big yellow folding marker to let all the male campers know she was inside. She put on her rubber gloves and started wiping mirrors and faucets and shower walls. She scrubbed the toilets and the urinal and mopped the floor. She changed the plastic bags in the trash cans and sprayed a deodorant spray before finally leaving.

She then moved over to the women's side and began the same ritual. Rose, a registered nurse by profession and a woman used to keeping things clean, did not mind the menial labor she did at Shady Grove. Since she was a little girl, she had always enjoyed the work of cleaning a room. It was the event of order that she liked, tasks that had a beginning and an ending and always achieved the desired results. What was filthy and messy became clean and tidy. What was chaotic and disorderly was suddenly made right. It had been the only means for surviving her childhood, her only way to get through her mother's death and her father's violence.

As a child, she cleaned because the chores were designated to her, being the only female in the home. She cleaned because she knew her father hated disorder and filth and she was always hopeful that if the house was clean enough, he wouldn't want to drink, wouldn't be driven to violence. It was, in fact, the only time her father ever seemed pleased with Rose. He usually found things she had not done correctly or completely, but on occasion, he would congratulate her for how well she polished a piece of silver or swept out a corner. Rose lived for those moments.

When she married she brought into her home the same sort of domestic drive she had developed as a young girl. Everything in her house was neat and ordered and her husband, like her father, would once in a while call attention to how neat Rose kept things. Having a clean and well-kept house was a great source of pride for her.

Rose sprayed cleaner on the mirror in front of the sinks and began wiping. She moved quickly, her hand spread across the paper towel, covering corner to corner, top to bottom. She stopped only once her reflection became clear. Her need for cleanliness and order was one of the reasons Rose had not wanted to have children when she was younger. She had heard lots of friends and acquaintances talking about the disarray and the disorder that were a natural result of motherhood and she knew that if she had children she would never be able to maintain the kind of order to which she had become accustomed.

There were other reasons for not being a parent, of course. She knew that she was afraid that somehow her own childhood would be repeated, a life of loss and disappointment handed down to a next generation. She was afraid that she would become either the absent mother or the heavy-handed parent she had been left with. She had chosen not to give birth because she was afraid of the kind of parent she would be. And then there was her marriage with Rip. It had only taken a few years of living with him before she understood that their relationship was tenuous enough on its own, and bringing in another person might stretch and ultimately break the fragile bond that they shared.

Rose looked closely at herself in the mirror, recognizing that as the years had passed the idea of having a child had just been pushed farther and farther away. Until Ms. Lou Ellen had spoken of Rose having a baby, Rose had not considered motherhood in a very long time. And yet, as she stared at her reflection there at Shady Grove, she knew that it hadn't taken much conversation about the idea of parenting to make her look again at her decision not to have a child. She couldn't say in complete confidence that she never wanted to be a mother. She couldn't look at herself and say truthfully that she wasn't at least a little curious about the idea, a little interested in what it would mean to be a mother. Ms. Lou Ellen had found a nerve, and now that it was struck, Rose was going to have to rethink the choice she had made. She finished cleaning the sinks and moved to the toilets and then the shower stalls.

Rose was wiping down the walls in the rear shower when she heard the main door open and close. She realized that she had not moved the cleaning sign over to the women's side. It was leaning against the wall outside. She finished the stall she was in and walked out of the shower area.

"Hey, I'm just about done," Rose said, shaking off her thoughts of Ms. Lou Ellen's predictions as she glanced up. She caught Chariot standing in front of the mirror in a blast of tears. "Oh, my." Rose dropped her bucket and went over to her. "Are you okay?" she asked.

The young girl wept and nodded. She reached over and pulled a piece of paper towel from the dispenser. "I didn't know anybody was in here," she said, trying to hold back her emotion.

"Just me," Rose responded. "Here"—she walked over and pulled some toilet tissue from the holder—"this is softer. I make sure we use the good stuff."

Chariot smiled and wiped her eyes and nose. She shook her head. "I'm sorry, I just needed to have a moment. I'm in such a mess."

"Messes are just fine here," Rose announced.

The young woman nodded gratefully as she wiped her face. "Rhonda told you about Jason?"

Rose nodded. She waited.

"Have you made dinner plans for the evening?" she asked.

"Rhonda and Lucas are going to church," Chariot replied, smoothing her hair back with her fingers. "They invited me, but I just didn't feel like being in a group. They said that they would check on me when they got back. I thought maybe I'd just go into town and get a burger."

Rose knew that Rhonda and Lucas went to an evening Bible study at their church when they were in town. She also knew that they could be very late getting back.

"Well, look, why don't you come over to my boyfriend's place with me?" Rose asked. "He's fixing me dinner and I know there will be enough for an extra person."

Chariot shook her head. "I don't want to be any trouble," she said.

"No trouble," Rose responded, thinking about that word *trouble* again and how often it had been used that day. "I'll just finish my work and then change my clothes and we'll walk over together. Were you going to take a shower?" she asked, noticing the towel and other belongings the young girl had placed on the bench by the bathroom door.

Chariot nodded. "I fell asleep this afternoon after putting up the tent and now I'm just a grimy mess. I can't wait to clean up."

Rose smiled. "I understand," she noted. "Why don't I just meet you at your campsite in about thirty minutes?"

Chariot nodded, agreeing that would give her enough time to get cleaned up. They said good-bye and Rose left the facility. By the time she returned the cleaning supplies back in the closet at the office, parked the golf cart, and walked to her travel trailer, she only had fifteen minutes to change her clothes and call Thomas to make sure it was okay that Chariot joined them. When she flipped open her cell phone she noticed that she had a message.

It was Thomas. He had called while she was cleaning to say that he had been called away. Rose understood that to mean that the recovering alcoholic that he was sponsoring had contacted him and needed Thomas's support. She had become used to those kinds of phone calls and interruptions in their plans. She never really minded though because she understood how helpful her boyfriend was to so many people. Thomas had also said that the dinner was ready and waiting in the oven and that all she would need to do was warm things up. He had suggested that she go ahead and eat without him.

"Perfect," she said to herself, realizing that would give her time to ask Chariot all of the questions she wanted to ask. She could find out for herself what had happened back in Pierre.

She dressed and walked over to the tent, where she noticed a lantern shining inside. "Knock, knock," she said, since there wasn't really any other way to let the girl know that she was outside.

"Hey, Rose, come on in," she said, opening the flap to the tent. "I just need to put on my shoes," she said.

Rose bent down and walked in. She glanced around at the setup. She noticed the duffel bag of clothes, the Coleman lantern, and a picture in a small frame on a metal fold-up table, the sleeping bag unrolled and blankets and a pillow on top placed along the rear of the tent. It appeared as if Chariot had everything that she needed for her camping comfort.

"Looks like you have all the right stuff for tent camping," Rose noted with a smile.

Chariot was pulling on her sneakers. "Yeah, Jason had packed the car with all of this before he woke me up," she said. "We camp a lot in the summer." She hesitated. "We used to camp a lot," she corrected herself.

Rose nodded. She studied the young woman as she tied her shoelaces.

"Where were you going?" Rose asked, trying not to pry too much so soon, but curious about what the couple had been planning before the murder occurred.

Chariot finished, stood up, and shook her head. "I don't know," she replied. "Jason woke me up in the middle of the night, pulled me out of bed, and told me to get ready. I had been asleep maybe two or three hours. I don't think he had even gotten into bed. We hadn't planned to go anywhere."

She threw on a light jacket and then walked over to the door of the tent. She held open the flap and Rose walked out first.

"I've tried and tried to figure out what he was thinking or where he was going to take us," she explained. She bent down to zip the flap, closed it, and then stood up.

"Which way?" she asked Rose.

Rose pointed in the direction of Thomas's place and they began walking past the campground.

"He was involved with some guys," Chariot said. She was hesitant to speak, but appeared glad to finally have someone to talk to. "He got a phone call a couple of weeks ago. And he started acting strange after that."

Rose waited for more.

"Anyway, he didn't seem to like them very much and he had told me that he just had to do this one thing with them and then he'd never have to see them again."

The two women walked down the path. The sun was setting

and Rose glanced over to see the colors as they fell across the river. She loved the Mississippi at this time in the evening.

"You don't know what the one thing was?" Rose asked.

Chariot shook her head. There was a pause.

"I think it was a robbery, though."

"What makes you think that?" The idea surprised Rose.

The girl shrugged. "Jason had done some time for breaking and entering a few years ago. He was good at picking safes and I think he had to pull this last job to get these guys to leave us alone," she explained. "I sometimes overheard their conversations."

"Do you know what they stole?" Rose asked, thinking that might have something to do with the murder.

Chariot shook her head. "I just think they found somebody rich," she said. "I heard him say something about 'the president,'" she added. "And I think it was just cash, easy cash, I heard him say once."

Rose looked confused. "The president?" she asked. "Why would they call somebody that?"

Chariot shrugged. "Pierre is the state capital," she said. "I think it was somebody in politics. They have all the money in South Dakota," she added. "Them and the ranchers. I just think they were breaking into a house of some rich politician and I think Jason opened the safe. I think that he must have found out something about the other guys or maybe he took something he shouldn't have and they killed him."

"This is it," Rose said as she pointed to the driveway of Thomas's trailer.

They headed to the front door. It was unlocked and they

walked inside. The lights were on and there was a note on the table that read, "Enjoy! I'll be back as soon as I can." And then he had signed his name. Rose noticed that there were two place settings and she decided just to let Chariot sit at the place Thomas had set for himself.

She gestured for the young woman to sit at the table and Rose began making the preparations for their dinner. Like he had said in his message, everything was already done. She just turned on the stove to heat up the garden peas. The roast was still warm as she pulled it out of the oven and placed it on the trivet on the table. She put the potatoes in the microwave and fixed the glasses with ice and tea. She found some bread already in a basket and she put everything in front of Chariot.

"This looks so good," Chariot said. "I haven't had a real meal to eat in a while."

"Well, dig in," Rose said. And the two of them started their evening meal.

"Pot roast was Jason's favorite," the young woman noted.

Rose watched the tears fill her eyes. She leaned over and squeezed her on the arm. They paused and then kept eating.

"Rhonda said that you saw the guy who shot Jason," Rose said. "She said that you were with him at the apartment when the killer was there." She was passing the bread basket over to Chariot. She wondered if she was pushing too hard.

Chariot nodded without seeming to mind the questions. "I saw him as he left. I just saw his back. He was on a bike," she noted. "I also saw him on the road before I got to Huron."

"Did he see you?" Rose asked.

Chariot shook her head. "But he's looking for me," she added.

Rose waited for more.

"Jason told me before he died that they thought I was at work and that I had it, or something like that." She took a bite of roast beef. "Jason was the one who told me to leave. He thought I was in danger. Then when I was driving out of town, I saw the guy on the road following me," she added. "I know it was the same guy."

"What do you think Jason meant, that you *had* it?" Rose asked. She took a sip of tea. "Do you think he had taken something from somebody or had something this guy wanted?"

Chariot shrugged. "I don't know," she replied. "He never told me anything that he had stolen. And I've looked everywhere in the car and in the stuff he packed. I haven't found anything that looks important or different or anything that somebody would want." She continued to eat.

"Did you know these other guys that he was with?" Rose asked.

Chariot shook her head. "Not really. Jason never mentioned their names, but I think I know who they are. I thought maybe I should try and contact them, see if they know anything; but I'm afraid they're the ones behind Jason's murder." She put down her fork, appearing a bit distressed at the conversation.

Rose thought about the story that she was hearing. She guessed that Chariot's boyfriend had been murdered because of something he had done with this group of guys. It made sense that he had taken something from the house that they robbed or that he had threatened to go to the police about the others. She wondered about Jason, about what had happened on the night he was killed. And she was still curious about the young woman's path from Pierre to West Memphis, Arkansas.

"Did you stop somewhere else in South Dakota before coming here?" Rose asked, still pushing Chariot.

Chariot nodded. "I went to my grandma's," she replied. "She has this way of helping me see clear," she said. "She was really more of my mother than my real one," she added. "But I saw my mama, too."

"Chariot, did you bring that paper from South Dakota, the one that was in the recycling bin?" Rose asked, wondering if the young woman understood that she was listed as wanted by the police.

Chariot looked confused. She thought about the question. "I purchased a paper before I left Mitchell yesterday. I never read it, though," she said. "Why? Did you read it or something?" she asked.

Rose could tell that Chariot did not fully understand her situation, that she had not read the paper at all. "Then you don't know, do you?" she asked.

Chariot dropped her hands in her lap and looked intently at Rose. "Know what?" she asked.

Rose was just getting ready to explain the charges that were being held against her back in her home state when they both were startled at what they heard. Police sirens were blaring and they were heading in the direction of Shady Grove.

ELEVEN

What's going on?" Rose asked Lou Ellen after she had walked up to where everyone was standing.

She had convinced Chariot to stay at Thomas's while she went to the office to find out what had happened. Once they heard the sirens, Chariot had immediately jumped up to run, explaining that it was a policeman who had killed Jason, that she had seen him following her while she was still in South Dakota.

She was getting ready to run out the door, certain that the policeman-murderer had found her, that he was driving into the campground, creating a lot of commotion, calling a lot of attention to himself and his authority, but that he was there for her, to take her into custody and kill her.

Rose was confused by Chariot's story and knew she needed some time to sort through everything. She explained that she needed to go and check on things and she thought that she had convinced the girl to stay where she was and give Rose the chance to find out who was at the office and why they were there. She tried to calm Chariot by saying that the arrival of police officers at Shady Grove could be something completely unrelated to her and her situation and tried to persuade her just to wait until she found out what was going on. Rose assumed Chariot was obeying her instructions.

Rose walked the length of the path trying to figure out what she would say when she got to the office, if in fact the police were there for Chariot. A policeman had killed her boyfriend. Rose knew it would be difficult to protect her. She wasn't sure what she was going to say if the sheriff was indeed looking for her. Even though she hated the thought of telling Sheriff Montgomery where the young fugitive was hiding, she also understood the great penalty involved in failing to disclose the whereabouts of someone in trouble with the law.

Rhonda and Lucas were on their way back to Shady Grove and if they had seen the parade of police cars coming into their campground, Rose hoped that she would find them at the office before she arrived. When she got to the steps of the empty office, she realized that the Boyds were still in town at their church meeting. She was going to have to manage this crisis by herself.

She walked over to where two patrol cars were parked, just at the campground entrance, and found Sheriff Montgomery and two deputies standing outside talking to Ms. Lou Ellen. Rose took in a deep breath and pretended not to be worried or upset by their presence.

"It seems they think we have a murderer in our midst,"

Ms. Lou Ellen announced, stepping over to Rose. She had been standing in the path with her dog, Lester Earl, blocking the cars. The officers were standing by their cars; Sheriff Montgomery and one deputy by the first one, and a very young officer standing alone at the driver's side of the second vehicle.

Rose couldn't see below his waist, but noticed that he seemed particularly nervous. She wondered if he had his hand on his gun.

Ms. Lou Ellen had already put on her robe and pajamas, a matching silk set with large red roses set against a background of rich emerald-green. Ms. Lou Ellen loved her nightclothes and she had some beautiful sets of pajamas. Rose noticed this particular outfit and even remembered when it had arrived with the mail one evening, a purchase from some catalogue.

Rose glanced at her watch and noticed that it was after 8:00 P.M. and that Ms. Lou Ellen's attire was actually quite appropriate, even if it did seem to make the sheriff a bit uncomfortable. The dog snarled a bit at Montgomery.

Ms. Lou Ellen reached down and petted her dog and then shook her head at the three officers and spoke loudly enough for them to hear her. "Thank you, Lester Earl," she said to the dog.

And then she spoke to Rose. "I told them that if that was the case, that a murderer was in our midst, I would have certainly read it in my horoscope this morning and called them first to report it, but they didn't seem too interested in my opinion."

Rose glanced over at Sheriff Montgomery who was walking closer to her.

"Rose," he said as a greeting. He nodded.

"Sheriff," she said with a smile. "What's all the racket about? Are you trying to hurt our business?" she asked.

They both looked toward the river to see the campers standing outside their rigs, curious about all of the commotion. A few of them were walking toward the office. Old Man Willie, one of the full-time campers who lived at Shady Grove, had left his trailer and was standing behind the office listening. He didn't seem to want to come too close, but he was certainly curious.

Sheriff Montgomery shook his head. "Look, I know she's here," he said without addressing her concern about the others in the campground. "Chariot Stevens, age twenty-two. I need to take her in. She's wanted in Pierre for the murder of her boyfriend."

"Twenty-two years old?" Rose said, sounding surprised. "What would a twenty-two-year-old girl be doing camping in West Memphis?"

Montgomery studied Rose. "I knew something was up with you-all this afternoon. I just didn't put my finger on it until I went over to visit Jimmy at his station. He mentioned the girl again, said she was real skittish-acting and then I took a look at the surveillance video at the station. And I agreed with him. Something just didn't seem right. So I decided to run her South Dakota plates. And then, well, we know what I found then."

"Sheriff, I thought you were softening up. Do you really enjoy making trouble for people?" Rose asked.

"That's a fine question," Ms. Lou Ellen chimed in, stepping close to Rose, forming a kind of alliance. "Leon, I bet you're a

Scorpio, aren't you?" She eyed him closely. "Scorpios are like unexploded bombs, just waiting to go off. They're always planning something to do," she explained. "Sounds like you." Her voice was strong, but managed just the right tone of sweetness. She held the robe together under her chin with one hand on top of the other.

He waved her off without answering. Ms. Lou Ellen just smiled.

"I knew it," she said, taking his silence to be her confirmation that she was right. "Three moons in your Saturn and you question every detail in life." She was studying the lawman. "Or maybe you're a Cancer. Do you feel let down about everything?"

"Where's the girl?" he asked Rose, still ignoring the older woman's astrological reading.

"Who?" Rose asked, trying to appear as if she wasn't understanding him.

"Look, Rose, I know she's here. I saw her at her tent when I left a few hours ago. I drove past her campsite on my way out that side road. I saw her car. I recognized the automobile in the video." He sighed, growing more and more impatient with the women blocking his way. "Is she at her tent?" he asked.

Rose shrugged. "Let's just go inside and I'll check the reservation log," she said. She turned to walk to the office. "What did you say her name was?" she asked. And then, "Aren't you supposed to have a search warrant before you come blasting up on private property demanding to bother our guests?" She figured that would be something that Mary might say and she thought it sounded good.

"I've already talked to Rhonda and Lucas," he explained, his voice sounding restless and tired. He didn't follow her up the steps to the office, just remained standing in the path in front of Ms. Lou Ellen.

Rose turned around and looked first at Ms. Lou Ellen and then at the sheriff. The older woman rolled her eyes as if there was nothing else to be done.

"Where are Rhonda and Lucas?" Rose asked, surprised that her friends would have confessed such a thing to the sheriff and then not get here first to explain things to everyone, especially Chariot. She suddenly felt disappointed in the two people she admired the most.

"They've gone to fetch Lionel Kearns," Montgomery replied.

Rose nodded, suddenly understanding that they were doing the right thing. They were lining up an attorney for Chariot.

Lionel Kearns was a good man and a very good lawyer, the best defense lawyer in West Memphis. He had been a friend of the Boyds for a long time and he would be more helpful than anyone for the camper from Pierre, South Dakota.

Even if they didn't know the news that Chariot had just told Rose—that a policeman was the real murderer—Rose realized that Rhonda and Lucas were smart to think of contacting a lawyer and cooperating. They understood that the sheriff was a reasonable person and that he wouldn't hurt Chariot, but that he would not be turned away or sidetracked. He was a very efficient lawman. They also understood that they really had no choice other than to tell the truth and to help the sheriff obey the law and deal with the charges Chariot faced back in South

Dakota. Hiring a lawyer was the best thing they could do in this situation.

Montgomery had met Rhonda and Lucas as they were coming out of church, had been kind enough to wait until after the service and generous enough to tell the campground owners before he conducted the official business of picking up Chariot.

He had explained to them about the police report he had received over the wire. Murder was a serious allegation. He knew when he saw the girl's picture and a description of the car she was driving that it was the girl who had been seen at Jimmy Novack's service station. When he ran her plates and got the report, he knew what had to be done.

"She's just a kid, Leon," Rose said, coming back down the steps and trying to soften the man a bit.

"She's also wanted by the state police in South Dakota. I have to take her in," he explained.

Rose blew out a breath and folded her arms across her chest. "She's up at Thomas's. We were eating dinner," she said. "Just stay here and I'll go get her."

Sheriff Montgomery considered the idea. In spite of everything he and Rose had been through together, all of her meddling in police business with the murder of Lawrence Franklin almost two years earlier and then the man from New Mexico who had been murdered at Shady Grove, he trusted Rose. He liked her and he knew she meant no harm. He chewed on the inside of his bottom lip and narrowed his eyes at her.

"No monkey business," he said. "You go get her and bring her right to me," he instructed. "You can let her get her personal things from her tent if she needs anything," he added. "No need to bring too much though, it'll just be confiscated when we get to the station."

Rose nodded. "Yes, sir," she said. "Thank you," she added.

"Just do the right thing," he said and stepped out of her way.

"Okay," she replied. "Do you think you could shut off the lights?" she asked. She turned to look at the two cars behind them, the blue lights still swirling. "And is he going to shoot anybody?" She gestured toward the deputy at the last car.

"Martin, take your hand off of your weapon!" he yelled.

"Now, that's something I have always wanted to say," Ms. Lou Ellen said. She winked at the sheriff when he turned around to face her.

Sheriff Montgomery shook his head and looked around again at his deputies. He lifted his chin toward the cars and the deputy at the front car leaned inside and turned the lights off. The deputy then walked over to the second vehicle and did the same thing. Rose watched as the young man stood up from the car in the rear and raised his head as if he understood the purpose of their arrival had been completed.

"Just bring her here," the sheriff said again to Rose.

Rose nodded and began moving down the path to Thomas's trailer.

"Find out her sign," Ms. Lou Ellen instructed her. Rose turned to her friend and rolled her eyes.

"We might discover something important," she said.

"Okay," Rose finally said and started walking down the path.

Rose moved slowly in the direction of Thomas's trailer. She

thought about how drastically this young woman's world had changed in the last few days. Her boyfriend had been involved in some sort of shady arrangement, she had seen him die, she had been followed by the murderer who she said was an officer of the law, and now, she was being charged with homicide.

Rose realized that in all of her bad times—the affair that Rip had, the rocky and difficult relationship she had with her father, the legendary police captain Morris Burns, the early death of her mother when Rose was so young, even in all of those difficult circumstances—she had never had to deal with what the young Chariot Stevens was getting ready to face.

Rose walked in the darkness, the path lit only by the new evening moon and a few distant stars, and wondered about this mystery camper at Shady Grove. She wondered how well Rhonda and Lucas really knew her, if the story she was telling them was true.

Maybe, Rose thought as she moved away from the office, the girl was guilty. Maybe everything she was telling them at Shady Grove was a lie. Maybe she came home from work and there had been some argument with her boyfriend, some fight over money or another woman, maybe even a baby, even though she had told Rhonda that she wasn't pregnant, and in the heat of that moment Chariot had shot and killed her boyfriend.

Rose shook away her doubts about Chariot. She knew that there was something Chariot wasn't telling, some secret, but Rose didn't think it was that she had murdered Jason. Rose trusted that the young friend of Rhonda and Lucas was telling them the truth and Rose was going to continue to try and help her as much as she could.

After all, she thought as she made the turn up the driveway that led to Thomas's trailer, she had been trusted and believed when she arrived at Shady Grove. Even when the sheriff was questioning Rose about her interest in the death of a local funeral home owner, Thomas, Rhonda, Lucas, Mary, and Ms. Lou Ellen had never doubted her, had never been suspicious of her.

Rose remembered the extravagant hospitality and acceptance she had received when she was first a camper at Shady Grove and she understood that she had to offer that same kindness and acceptance to Chariot. She would support her in whatever way she could.

When she opened the front door, Rose was startled to find Thomas sitting at the table in his usual spot—the very place Chariot had been sitting when Rose had left—eating dinner. He looked up and smiled and then immediately seemed to sense that something was wrong.

"Where is she?" Rose asked, glancing around the room and starting to feel a little nervous.

"Where is who?" Thomas replied.

"Chariot," Rose said.

Thomas shrugged and then shook his head. "There was nobody here when I got home."

And Rose stepped forward, slumped in the chair across from him, and dropped her face in her hands.

"We've got trouble," was all she said.

TWELVE

Rose headed up the path away from Thomas's trailer and toward the highway. She sent Thomas to look for Chariot down near the river. Rose figured that it took her about thirty minutes to walk to the office, have her conversation with the sheriff, and then walk back to Thomas's. She assumed Chariot hadn't gotten too far. Rose wondered if Chariot went back to her tent, but she decided that the young woman had probably headed in the direction of the interstate. She guessed that Chariot had assumed the police were there for her and she had run off on her own.

Rose walked on and realized that she did feel a little angry that Chariot hadn't obeyed her. She was a bit perturbed that the young woman hadn't stayed where she was, but had instead, taken off. She softened a bit, however, when she considered that Chariot was afraid and she had no real reason to trust Rose. They had, after all, only just met.

Rose hurried along the path in the dark. She stumbled a bit, but she managed not to fall. She called out Chariot's name a few times, but she never heard a response. She knew the dirt path was about four miles before it intersected with a paved road that led to Highway 55. She moved on, wishing she had worn better walking shoes, and wondering if this was even the direction that Chariot had taken.

"Girl, where on earth did you go?" Rose asked out loud, not expecting an answer. She walked along the path, shaking her head.

"Help." It was a faint cry.

Rose stopped to listen. "Hello?" she called out.

There was nothing.

"Chariot, is that you?" Rose asked.

"I think I'm hurt." The voice came from the woods.

"Chariot?" she called again.

"I fell down," the voice replied.

Rose headed in the direction of where she thought she had heard the voice. She moved to her left. She stepped through the tall grass and into the edge of the woods. When she got to the first row of trees, she looked to her right and saw Chariot sitting on the ground holding her right foot. Rose dropped down beside her.

"What happened?" Rose asked.

"I was running and I just slipped and fell," Chariot replied.

"Let me look," Rose said. She felt around Chariot's foot and ankle. "Does this hurt?" she asked as she examined her.

"Yes," Chariot responded, wincing. "Maybe it's broken," she added.

"Well, maybe," Rose replied. She sighed. She probed a bit more and felt the ankle swelling, but did not notice any bones protruding through the skin or any other signs of a fracture. "I think maybe you just sprained it," she said, slowly releasing Chariot's foot. "We should get it looked at though," she noted.

Chariot didn't respond.

"Why did you run off?" Rose asked.

Chariot dropped her face and shook her head. "I just got scared," she replied.

Rose sighed. She stood up and looked around to see if anyone had followed her. She wondered how long the sheriff would wait before coming to search for the missing girl.

"I've always run," Chariot said softly. "As long as I can remember." She leaned against the tree. "From my daddy when he would beat my mama, from my mama when she finally killed him, from bad relationships and places where I wasn't accepted. It's what I know best. I always run," she repeated.

Rose waited before responding. She dropped her arms by her side and then she squatted down beside Chariot and leaned against the tree, too. She was surprised by Chariot's honesty, but she understood what the young woman was saying. Rose had developed her own habit of running away from things after her mother died. It became the way she also handled everything. Rose knew that she had spent her lifetime trying to get somewhere other than where she was, always trying to get away from something—the loneliness, the abuse, the anger, she was never sure. She just knew that escape was a coping mechanism that she was familiar with.

"I have a little girl," Chariot suddenly announced. "I quit running when I had her."

Rose turned to look at Chariot. She was surprised by the news. She didn't respond.

"I'm supposed to have custody of her in a few months." She stopped. "I mean, I was going to have custody of her," she said. "Now, I'll probably never see her again."

Rose couldn't see her, but she could hear Chariot begin to cry. She reached over and took the girl by the hand.

"Tell me what happened," Rose said.

Chariot waited and then began. "I was in trouble a lot," she said, wiping her face. "I got messed up with drugs and running around with the wrong crowd. And then I got pregnant and I wanted to be clean for the baby. For the first time in my life, I really cared about somebody other than myself and something other than just trying to get away."

Rose nodded. She thought about the conversation she had had with Ms. Lou Ellen about Rose being a mother. She thought again about motherhood, wondering how it would feel if she suddenly discovered she was pregnant. She wondered if it would have a calming effect on her like it did on Chariot.

"Jason and me were going to get married and find a nice place to live in Pierre. I had a baby shower and had a good job. Everything was finally coming together for us. And then, it fell apart. I got arrested for something I had done a long time ago, something I was told had been dismissed. But it turned out to be this case that had to do with some big drug deal and everybody involved got prison time. I gave birth at the infirmary and right after she was born they let me hold her a few hours and then they took her away, gave her to foster parents." Chariot took a breath.

Rose did not respond. She could only imagine the pain of having a child taken away from her.

"She's been in the same home since she was born. The foster mother is real nice and she lets me see her a lot. She brought her to prison and sent me pictures. And I only had to serve two years. And then I was told that if I showed that I could get a job and stay clean, that if I kept my appointments with my parole officer and took some parenting classes, and if I didn't leave the city of Pierre, I could get Constance. Have her with me."

Rose waited for the rest. But there was nothing more said. Chariot grew silent and Rose finally understood that not only had Chariot lost her boyfriend, by fleeing South Dakota, the young woman had also lost rights to the custody of her daughter. Suddenly, the secret that Rose had guessed about was out in the open. Chariot was a mother and this mother had lost her child.

"You can still get custody of your daughter," Rose said, trying to sound optimistic. "We just need to get this mess cleared up."

"I just don't think it's that easy," Chariot responded. "If the police think I killed Jason, I got no chance to get Constance back. They'll make sure I never see my little girl again."

The two women sat for a few minutes in silence. Rose was trying to figure out what they should do. Even with the new information about a baby, Rose knew that the sheriff was still waiting for them at the office. And she knew he wouldn't wait much longer. She also knew that if he thought Chariot had run, he'd be harder on her and less likely to believe her story about a police officer being involved.

Rose knew that Chariot's injury was not too serious, but that it would prohibit them from being able to walk too far. She thought it might be best if Chariot just stayed where she was, but with all that had happened, she didn't really want to leave her alone. She was standing up when she noticed headlights coming in their direction. Someone was driving toward them, coming from the interstate. Chariot saw the lights, too.

"Just stay here," Rose whispered to Chariot.

The truck rolled beside them and stopped. Rose waited and then stepped out of the woods.

"You need a ride?" the voice from inside the truck called out.

Rose peered closely at the vehicle, trying to see if she recognized it or the driver. She felt a bit nervous and motioned again for Chariot to stay hidden behind the tree. She studied the truck and waited to respond.

She leaned closer and then suddenly smiled.

"What you doing out here, Willie?" she asked.

The old man grinned. "Just driving around in the moonlight," he replied.

Rose leaned down and reached for Chariot. She pulled the injured girl up from her seat and helped her walk down the embankment toward the truck. Old Man Willie opened the driver's door and jumped out to help the women.

"Miss," he said with a nod, greeting Chariot.

Chariot stopped and glanced at the man standing before her. "I know you," she said.

Rose turned to Willie. She was surprised that Chariot would have met one of the other campers at Shady Grove.

The old man didn't look at either woman. He simply helped Rose get Chariot to the truck, opened the door on the passenger's side, and helped her in.

"You chased down the papers when that wind came when I was setting up camp. You caught one, the most important one," Chariot recalled as she slid across the seat.

"He found the birth certificate for Constance. He caught it and brought it to me," she reported to Rose, who was getting into the truck beside her.

"He came in the wind," Chariot said to Rose.

Willie didn't reply. He shut the door and walked around the truck to get in.

"Willie," he said as a means of introducing himself. "My name is Willie."

"Chariot," she responded to him. "Chariot Stevens."

"How did you know where to find us?" Rose asked, assuming that he was looking for them when he drove down the path in her direction.

He shook his head. "Not too many places to run down by the river," he explained.

Rose nodded as if she understood, but she was still curious as to why Old Man Willie knew to look for them. She tried to remember if she saw him at the office when she had met with the sheriff and then realized that didn't really matter at that moment.

She took in a breath and turned to Chariot. The truck didn't move. Willie seemed to be waiting for instructions.

"What do you want to do?" Rose asked.

"I guess I don't have a lot of choices," Chariot responded.

"Not with your injury," Rose noted. "I think you need to get it looked at," she added.

"I could run," Chariot said. "Nobody else knows where we are, do they?" She turned to Willie as if he might have an answer.

"I suspect they'll find you," he replied. "The sheriff's pretty good at his job. And Rose is right, you can't get far with that foot."

There was a pause as the truck's engine continued to idle.

"I don't know what to do," Chariot said, wondering how many times she had said that sentence in the last three days.

Rose shrugged. "I don't know, either," she responded.

"What about you, Mr. Willie?" Chariot asked, appearing as if she somehow trusted the man in the truck. "What would you do?"

Old Man Willie shook his head and paused. "I can't tell you that," he finally said. "I made too many messes of my own life to try and direct the path of somebody else's." He rested his hands on the steering wheel, looking straight ahead.

Chariot and Rose watched him. They both saw the weathered way he held himself, the wiry arms, his long skinny brown fingers. Chariot smiled when he reached into his back pocket and handed her a handkerchief. She took it from him and wiped her face.

"Thank you," she said, handing it back to him.

Rose studied the driver. She hadn't heard Willie say this many words the entire time she had been at Shady Grove. She was surprised that he was there, suddenly appearing out of nowhere, and she was also surprised that he was talking so much.

"Just keep it," he said. And then he turned first to Rose and then to Chariot.

Chariot nodded.

"I trust them at Shady Grove," he said.

His words surprised Rose again. She and Chariot listened.

"I was in trouble a lot," he confessed and turned away, placing his hands back on the steering wheel as if that steadied him. "And they always took me in." He nodded. "Always saw the right thing for me," he added.

Rose watched as Chariot followed his eyes and looked down the road ahead of her.

"I suspect if they know about things, they'll take care of you, too, even the sheriff. He's tough-minded, but he's fair and he won't let nobody hurt you," he said. "And you won't find no better friend than that woman sitting next to you." He nodded at Rose who smiled. He drew in a breath as if he was going to say something else, but he didn't. He just nodded and the two women could tell that he was done.

Rose let Chariot sit with the information. She didn't think there was anything else to add. Chariot was going to have to make her own decision about what to do. Rose was not going to force her to do anything.

"I have a little girl," Chariot said, sharing her news with Willie.

"Yep," the old man replied. "I figured you to be a mother."

Rose stared at Willie. She was amazed at the insight he had. She wondered why he had never talked to her like he was talking to Chariot.

"I'm afraid I've lost her," she said, reaching over and taking Rose by the hand.

"You know where she is?" he asked.

Chariot just nodded, not understanding why he was asking that question. "She's in a foster home, in South Dakota," she replied.

"Then it's okay," he responded as if he were delivering the most logical explanation there was. "You can't lose somebody as long as you know where she is."

Rose smiled. Chariot took in a deep breath, waited for a minute, and then made her announcement.

"Take me back then, Mr. Willie," she said. A lone tear snaked down her cheek. "Take me back to Shady Grove." She reached up and wiped away the tear.

Rose looked out the window as Willie put the truck in gear and headed to the campground.

THIRTEEN

Old Man Willie drove his old pickup down the path, past Thomas's trailer, past the cemetery that was now a memorial site given in memory of Lawrence Franklin, and past the row of trees where Chariot's tent was pitched. The path wound around and he moved ahead without saying a word. He drove slowly, methodically, hoping that the time he was taking would help Chariot and Rose prepare for what they were getting ready to face.

Chariot had asked if she could stop by her tent and when they pulled up beside her car, finally arriving at her tent, he told them to wait. He turned off the truck and stepped out from his side and then walked over to the passenger's side. He opened the door and held out his hand, helping out Rose and then Chariot. He moved with them as the two women walked to the tent.

Chariot walked gingerly, her ankle now as swollen and blue as a party balloon.

"You hurting?" Rose asked.

Chariot nodded as she leaned against Rose.

Willie unzipped and held open the flap of the tent while Chariot hopped in. Rose let go of her arm and let Chariot go in by herself. She decided to let the young woman have some privacy.

On the way to the campground office, Chariot had asked to stop at her makeshift residence so that she could collect a few things she wanted to take with her. She wanted to secure some items before she went the few extra yards up the path and turned herself in.

Rose and Willie waited, patiently and politely, as Chariot went inside and changed clothes, choosing something warmer and more comfortable. They heard her as she made a few noises to indicate she had twisted her foot in the wrong direction or put too much weight on it, but neither of them interrupted or stuck their head in to check on her. They decided that if she needed something she would let them know.

Chariot gathered her purse that Rhonda had retrieved from the service station and finally packed a small bag with a few personal items. She hobbled out of the tent, looking somewhat refreshed, and handed Willie the keys to her car, along with the little canvas bag. "Would you watch my stuff for me?" she asked.

Rose watched the two of them, still surprised at the apparent connection between them.

The old man nodded and took her keys, placing them in his pants pocket, and the bag, which he carefully placed in a space behind the seat in his truck. He opened the door and Rose helped Chariot back in the passenger's side. Willie then walked over to get in himself. He started up the engine, put it in gear, and drove toward the direction of the office.

"You okay?" Rose asked as the patrol cars and the group gathered around them came into sight.

Chariot nodded.

They pulled up just as Rhonda and Lucas were coming down the driveway from the other direction. Everyone turned toward the noise of the motorcycle engines. The loud roar of two Harleys called for more attention than Old Man Willie's pickup truck. The two patrol cars were still parked near the office, and the two officers and several people with them were standing around the office steps.

Sheriff Montgomery was just getting ready to go searching for Rose and Chariot when he glanced in the direction of the truck driving up. He eyed the driver for a minute, figuring it was just Willie wanting to hear what was going on. After realizing that the driver was not alone, however, he leaned back against the hood of his car and nodded. Willie pulled up next to him and stopped.

Rose, still unsure of what she was going to say to the sheriff, how she was going to explain where the girl had gone, was the first one out of the vehicle. She told Chariot to remain in the truck.

"I was just about to come looking for you," the sheriff called out.

Rose stepped toward the officer.

"That her?" he asked.

Rose nodded and turned back to the truck. Willie jumped

out and walked around to the passenger's side. He helped Chariot out and she leaned against him.

"Chariot Stevens," Sheriff Montgomery said as the girl hobbled toward him.

She nodded as she leaned against Willie, holding him by the hand.

"You're under arrest for the murder of Jason Holmes in Pierre, South Dakota," the sheriff continued.

At first, Rose noticed how surprised Chariot appeared. The words did seem harsh and final. Rose also understood that this was the way the murderer would be able to find Chariot. She understood that this was the easiest method in which he would be able to apprehend her. It made perfect sense.

Chariot nodded.

Montgomery walked behind her and Chariot dropped Willie's hand. She moved toward the patrol car, leaned against it, spreading her arms across it. It seemed to everyone there that she had been through this procedure before. The sheriff did a casual search for weapons and then placed handcuffs on her wrists.

"Okay," he said, as a way to let her know it was fine to turn around. He glanced down and saw the swollen ankle.

"You hurt yourself?" he asked.

Chariot nodded in response.

"You running somewhere?" he asked, studying her, waiting for her reply. He was about to guess as much when he had seen the two women in Willie's truck.

There was an awkward silence.

Rhonda and Lucas parked their bikes at the office and walked over to join them.

"She was coming here," Old Man Willie suddenly answered for her.

Rose looked surprised and glanced at the older man. She hadn't expected him to say anything to the sheriff. "Yeah," Rose added. She figured she could take it from there. "I was just getting ready to explain that I asked Willie to drive us here," she lied. "I called him because I thought it would be better for her not to walk. Chariot tripped over a tent peg when she was walking out."

Rose stood next to Chariot. Rhonda, Lucas, and Thomas were standing near them. Ms. Lou Ellen was still waiting by the office steps with the deputies. She seemed very deep in conversation with them. While everyone had been waiting for Rose to return with the fugitive, Ms. Lou Ellen had begun a discussion with the two lawmen about their zodiac signs. Even though the sheriff had told them to look out for Chariot, they were paying attention to what Ms. Lou Ellen was telling them. She was doing a kind of impromptu reading.

"What happened?" the sheriff asked Chariot.

"It's like Miss Rose said, she fell," Willie said, answering for Chariot. He turned to the sheriff. The story was for him more than anybody. "She tripped on a peg. Miss Rose called me on her cell phone."

Rose whipped out her phone from her pants pocket to show that she had it with her. She turned to Chariot and then Sheriff Montgomery. "Well, let her sit down, for goodness' sake."

She and Rhonda helped Chariot into the patrol car.

Willie was standing with them. "It's her ankle and I suspect she needs some ice on it right away."

Everybody studied the old man who lived at the campground. No one had ever seen him this engaged in a conversation. He was usually so quiet, so shy.

While Sheriff Montgomery, standing next to the group at the car, thought a minute about the situation, Rose quickly retrieved an ice pack from the office freezer. When she returned, Sheriff Montgomery was still considering what needed to be done.

"We'll go by the emergency room first," he announced, having made his decision. "Martin, Davis," he yelled to his deputies, who were enthralled in their conversation at the steps. "Let's go, you two."

The two men jumped up and headed over to where the others were standing. Ms. Lou Ellen, still in her red and green flowered robe, waved as they left.

"Brother Leon"—Lucas stepped over, having observed what was happening—"do you think the restraints are necessary?" he asked.

Chariot was handcuffed and sitting in the backseat of the patrol car. She was leaning forward and appeared very uncomfortable.

Sheriff Montgomery sighed. He helped pull the young woman from the seat and then reached behind Chariot and unlocked the handcuffs. She leaned back against the seat, rubbing her wrists.

"Read her her rights, Martin," the sheriff said to one of the deputies. In all of the excitement, he had forgotten to do so once it became clear that the girl was injured. The two deputies stopped and, suddenly, it became obvious to those watching that the new officer of the law had forgotten the Miranda rights required by law to be read to everyone placed under arrest. His face turned bright red and the other officer laughed.

"It's fine, young Virgo," Ms. Lou Ellen called to Deputy Martin. "Don't get flustered by authority. No need for anxiety or to feel as if you've been thrown into chaos. Just remember that you can do this," she added. She waved in his direction as she walked down the office steps.

"You have the right to remain silent," Martin began confidently, smiling at the older woman who had explained why the planets are life forces and are the tools humans live by, and that because the planets were in a particular position in relation to the place of his birth he often felt tense and upset by the happenings in his life.

"When will she be extradited?" Thomas asked the sheriff.

Montgomery shook his head. "I guess it'll be up to South Dakota," he replied. "They'll be the ones to come and get her."

"Did you tell them that she was here?" Rose asked.

"Yep," the sheriff said. "I made a call up there when I got the report from her plates." He hesitated.

"So, they're on their way?" Rose asked.

Sheriff Montgomery chewed on the inside of his lip. "No, they said to call back when I had her in custody." He folded his arms around his chest. "Apparently, they like their reports neat and tidy before they act upon them. I'm getting ready to call right now," he said, pulling out his cell phone.

"Wait!" Rose shouted.

Sheriff Montgomery glanced over at her. His look was part surprise and part fatigue.

"She said it was a policeman who killed her boyfriend," Rose announced. She thought the information was important. She knew that her explanation sounded far-fetched, was hard to believe, but she also understood the danger the young woman could be in if she was turned over to the man she claimed was the murderer.

Sheriff Montgomery looked shocked. "What?" he asked.

"I didn't get all the details," she explained. "I wasn't able to finish my conversation with her because you drove up. But that's what she said, just before I left her to come see you."

The sheriff shook his head. "Well, that's a powerful accusation to make," he responded.

"So is an accusation that says she killed her boyfriend," Rhonda chimed in.

Sheriff Montgomery scratched his chin and placed his cell phone back in his front shirt pocket. "I can't do much about matters as they stand now," he said. "I already made a report," he explained. "They already know Chariot Stevens has been identified here in West Memphis."

"Yeah, but it wasn't officially received," Rose said.

"The young lady needs the medical attention first," Thomas noted. He had moved to stand beside Rose.

"Why not just take her over to Memphis, find out what's exactly wrong with her foot, let her get the right treatment, and then make the call?" he asked.

Rose glanced over at Thomas. She was grinning at him. She was amazed at what a good team they were.

Sheriff Montgomery glanced around at the group gathered near him. He shook his head and blew out a long breath. "What is it with you people at Shady Grove?" He rolled his eyes at what he was deciding to do.

Rhonda, Lucas, Thomas, Rose, and Willie waited.

"All right, I'll take her over to the hospital and get her looked at and then I'll make the call to Pierre. Rose, since you're a medically trained professional, I'm going to let you ride with me over to Memphis and see if you can hear the rest of her story. In the meantime, I'll try to make some calls to see what exactly happened in South Dakota."

The group gave a collective sigh.

"I don't know why I let you-all get to me like this," he muttered, shaking his head as he strolled off in the direction of his vehicle.

"I'll let you know what I find out," Rose said to the others and then quickly followed behind him.

FOURTEEN

Y ou think that's the right thing, letting her ride back there with the perp?" Deputy Davis asked the sheriff. He had turned around in his seat and stared long and hard at Rose sitting with the unrestrained Chariot Stevens. He was not very happy about having to go all the way into Tennessee to take a fugitive to get medical care. He was an officer who thought a person wanted for a crime like murder ought not to have any special treatment. And he considered X-rays and pain pills to be special treatment.

"I said it was fine and that's the end of it," the sheriff replied. He knew letting Rose ride in the back with the fugitive was against protocol, but he figured Rose could get more information from her than he could. And in spite of Rose's tampering in previous cases, Montgomery trusted her. She had, after all, done what she had promised. She had brought the girl to him.

Deputy Martin, the newest employee in the sheriff's department, had been sent back to the station. Sheriff Montgomery didn't need both of the men going over to Memphis to wait with him in the emergency room so he just took Davis with him.

"Besides, what is she going to do?" Montgomery replied, looking in his rearview mirror to watch the two women behind him. "They're sitting in the backseat of a moving car," he added.

The deputy glanced around behind him, gave a kind of disapproving look at Chariot and Rose, and then turned to face the road ahead. He rolled down his window a bit. "It's warm tonight," he commented. And the two men chatted about the weather and about Arkansas football, always a favorite subject among lawmen from that particular state.

"How are you doing?" Rose asked Chariot, deflecting the animosity coming from the deputy.

"I'm okay," she responded.

Rose took in a deep breath. She knew that they didn't have a lot of time. She wasn't sure where to start with her questions, but she knew she had to start asking something.

"All right, Chariot, we have to find out everything we can if we're going to get you out of this. Tell me exactly what happened the night Jason woke you up, the night he was . . ." She paused. "Killed," she added, hating the way she had started the interview. She sounded more like an interrogating officer, like her father, than she did a friend or someone simply concerned.

Chariot leaned back hard against the car seat and closed her eyes. It was obvious to Rose that her ankle was hurting.

"I had fallen asleep," she began, going through the night as she had over and over again in her mind since leaving Pierre.

"Jason woke me up about four thirty. He was already dressed and he just told me that I had to get up and get ready to leave."

"Did he say why?" Rose asked.

Chariot shook her head. "He just said that we had to go, that he was real sorry, that he knew what it meant for me to leave, and that he promised to make it right, but that there was no choice, we had to get out of town."

"You mentioned that he had been acting strange or different during the days leading up to the night he was murdered, how so?"

"Something was wrong," Chariot replied. "I didn't know it at the time, but now I remember him doing some different things before that night," she added.

"Like what?" Rose asked. "What kind of things?"

"He just seemed real distracted about something. He acted like he used to act when he had a job he was doing." Chariot slumped further down in the seat. She winced with pain.

"Is the ice helping any?" Rose glanced down at the girl's ankle. She leaned over and readjusted the small ice pack that she had gotten from the office before they left Shady Grove.

"A little," Chariot replied.

Rose sat back in her seat. "Tell me about the night he was murdered."

Chariot sighed. She had not talked about the murder to anyone. "I didn't realize how much danger we were in. I was working the morning shift at the pancake house and when I came home, he wasn't there. I fell asleep and when I got up, he was just coming in the door." Chariot recalled the night. "He seemed real happy, different from before, like he had accomplished something important." She paused. "And there was something more, a couple of days before, he acted like he had gotten more than he hoped for or something."

"What makes you think that?" Rose asked.

"He just seemed happy and he made a lot of calls and he laughed one day when I came home from work and asked me wouldn't it be nice if my pancake diner days were over. I thought that was especially strange because neither one of us had much money," Chariot noted.

"Did you know this policeman that you saw leave your apartment, the one who shot Jason?" Rose kept pushing the girl to think about that night in Pierre. She knew that this was the guy who was framing Chariot and that they had to figure out who he was if they were going to get the charges dropped.

Chariot shook her head. "But I've seen guys like him before," she said. "When I did time in jail, they all acted like that, you know, real smart and like they ran the show. This guy, even though I just had a glimpse of him, I could tell he was just like those others."

"But he wasn't one of the guys that you figure was with Jason to do this robbery that you think he had to do?"

Chariot shook her head again. "Those guys were losers. And none of them would have had the guts to kill somebody."

Rose glanced up to see if the sheriff and the deputy were listening, but they seemed to be engaged in their own conversation. With the window rolled down on the passenger's side and with the police scanner on, Rose figured that it was hard to hear their conversation as they drove across the bridge to Memphis.

"Okay, let's think about whatever Jason had done with the group of guys," Rose said, thinking Jason's actions needed an explanation as well. "Do you have any idea when that happened? Was there ever anything in the news about a robbery or a break-in at a politician's house?" She remembered that Chariot had mentioned that she thought it was a rich or famous person. She had not asked Chariot why she had thought this and now she wondered about that notion.

Chariot tried to remember what she had seen in the news the week before she had left Pierre. "No, I don't recall anything." She paused. "That is odd, isn't it?" she noted. "I mean, that there was never anything said about somebody being robbed." She paused. "In Pierre, there isn't a lot of news, so it seems like that would have been all over the papers at least."

Rose nodded. "What about that name again, 'the president'? Any other ideas about that?"

Chariot shook her head.

"Who would Jason have agreed to rob?" Rose asked. "Maybe a rancher or some politician?"

Chariot sighed. She leaned her elbow on her knee and placed her chin in her hand. "I don't know. I just think it was some rich guy."

"And you think most of the rich people in Pierre are either the ranchers or those in the legislature?" Rose asked.

Chariot shrugged. "I never thought about who had money in Pierre." And then, suddenly, her eyes got big and she turned to

Rose. "The drug dealer," she announced. "That's who it is," she said.

"The president is a drug dealer?" Rose asked.

Chariot sat up in her seat. "I remember!" She shook her head. "It was this guy outside Pierre that ran a meth lab. He had a lot of money and I think I heard somebody call him something like that, the president or something, I can't remember. But I bet that's who it was!"

"Well, that might make sense as to why there was nothing in the news about a robbery, if it was a drug dealer, I mean." Rose considered this idea. "He probably wouldn't report anything stolen to the police, but—"

"He would definitely kill the guys who did it," Chariot interrupted Rose with the logical explanation.

The two women sat quietly, considering this possibility. It did make sense to Rose that Jason could have been involved in robbing a criminal. There was probably a large amount of money involved and there would be no police inquiry. It would have been extremely risky to rob a drug dealer, but obviously could have been very profitable.

"What about this thing Jason said they were looking for?" Rose asked, recalling what Chariot had said earlier in the evening about the moments before Jason was killed. "Do you think he was in a good mood after the robbery because he had something he thought could make him more money?"

Chariot thought about the question. "I don't know."

"Did you see him with anything different after the night you think he did the robbery?"

"It's like I said, I don't know what that could be," she said. "I've looked through everything that was in the car," she added. "And now that I think about it, I can't believe that Jason would be stupid enough to take something from a drug dealer. He knew those guys. He wasn't dumb like that," she said.

Rose shook her head. "But he did get involved to start with," she noted. "And maybe he thought he wouldn't get caught. Maybe he thought it was a perfect crime."

"There's no such thing," Chariot insisted.

"No, I guess not," Rose responded. "But why would he have been involved with these guys in the first place? I thought Jason was clean."

"I don't think he had any choice about the robbery," Chariot finally acknowledged.

"What does that mean exactly?" Rose asked.

Chariot shook her head. "I don't know anything for sure," she confessed. "I just think Jason was forced into participating."

Rose waited. She could tell that Chariot had more to say.

"Sometimes, you get in a position where you owe somebody something," she explained. "You know what I mean?" she asked.

Rose nodded. She did understand that.

"And people who use other people, they know that."

There was a hesitation.

"And these people they may wait months or years before they come back to make you return their favor. You might have been out of trouble for a long time, living clean and sober, like me and Jason were, but they always come back. And they always expect you to hold up your end of the deal." Chariot glanced out the window. Her shoulders sagged and it appeared as if she was very clear about this part of her story. She seemed to have a very good handle on why her boyfriend did what he did.

"What was the favor he got?" Rose asked, thinking that Chariot probably knew that, too. "You said that on that night he woke you up that Jason told you that he was sorry about what it meant to leave town," she added. "What did he mean by that?" she asked.

Chariot didn't answer at first. She fidgeted with her hair, taking it out of the ponytail style she had been wearing, smoothing down the sides again, and then pulling it back up.

"He got me the chance to get Constance back," she finally confessed. "When I was in prison," she added.

The news surprised Rose. She waited for more.

"After she was born," Chariot explained, "they were going to take my baby away for good, send her somewhere else, another state or something." She shook her head. "I never understood exactly how he did it, but Jason got Constance in the foster care system in Pierre. He found somebody that pulled some strings and she didn't leave the state, and like I told you earlier, I got to see her, and I was just about to get full custody of her."

Rose watched as the tears rolled down the young woman's cheeks. She reached in her pocket to see if she had a tissue. She found one and handed it to Chariot. "How old is she?" Rose asked.

"Almost three," came the answer. "I didn't show you before, but I have a picture of her." She reached down and pulled out the purse she had been able to bring with her. She retrieved a small plastic bag with a few pictures inside and pulled one out.

"This was just a few weeks ago," she explained. "I got to see her three times a week, supervised, of course. The foster mother is still the same person as the one who got her when she was born.

Rose took the photograph and studied the little girl dressed in a pink jacket and a pink pair of jeans. She was smiling and holding out a flower, a small plastic flower, her smile wide with delight.

"She's definitely a cutie," Rose responded, looking a long time before handing back the picture to the young mother.

Chariot nodded. "I named her Constance because Jason and me, we felt like she made us different, made us want to be better always, you know, not just for a little while, but always."

Rose nodded. She wondered if Chariot's fears of losing custody were valid. She wondered what murder charges did to a custody suit. "We'll get her back for you," Rose said, not even sure why she said the words. She had no way at all of promising such a thing. She understood that had been Jason's promise, too, at one time and that Chariot had foolishly believed that as well.

Chariot looked closely at Rose and then turned away. "I think I've always known I'd never be good enough to keep her," she confessed.

Rose snapped up her head. "Wait a minute," she said. "Even if you lose custody, even if you broke the rules by leaving South Dakota and they keep her in the foster home a while longer, that doesn't mean that you aren't good enough to keep her." She shook her head.

Chariot put the photograph away without a response.

"Chariot, do you hear what I'm saying?" Rose asked. She spoke so loudly that the sheriff looked back at the two women from the rearview mirror.

They were just heading into Memphis.

"Everything all right back there?" the sheriff asked.

Rose, seeing his face in the mirror, nodded.

Chariot dropped her head.

"Do you hear what I'm saying?" she asked her again, reaching over and taking Chariot's chin in her hand. "Do you love Constance?" she asked.

"With all my heart," Chariot replied. "I've never loved anybody as much as I love her. She got me clean. She makes me want to stay clean."

"Then you are good enough to take care of her, you are good enough to bring her into your home," Rose said. She wiped Chariot's tear as it fell.

"Okay?" she asked.

"Okay," Chariot answered.

Rose pulled away and breathed out a big breath. "Now, here's what we have to do," she said. She sounded confident and certain of herself. "Lucas will try to find out the names of the other guys that were involved in the robbery. You got any idea about them?"

Chariot considered the question. "I think it was some guys from the bar where Jason used to hang out before we went to jail. I don't really know their names."

Rose nodded. She figured that Lucas could find out who those guys were.

"We'll work on that. Rhonda and Lucas are getting you squared away with a lawyer. I'm going to get Thomas to try and figure out who 'the president' is, try to look up on the Internet any news stories about meth labs in Pierre and who was running them, and I'm going to go through all of your stuff to see if there's anything that looks like it could be something somebody else would want. You need to try and remember everything about Jason in the last couple of weeks, everything he said or did that seemed out of the ordinary."

She took another breath as they pulled into the parking lot at the Baptist Hospital in Memphis.

"And we have to get him"—she gestured toward the sheriff—"to refrain from calling the police in South Dakota to report that he has you in custody since somewhere in Pierre there is a dirty cop."

"How are you going to do that?" Chariot asked.

"A lot of begging and a little bit of Southern charm," Rose replied.

She shook her head as she glanced in the direction of the sheriff. She wasn't sure that was going to work. "Is there anything else you can think of that we can do at Shady Grove?" she asked.

Chariot thought for a minute as the car stopped in front of the emergency room. There was something that she wanted to ask.

"I couldn't find my photo album," she said. "When I stopped by the tent with you and Mr. Willie to get some stuff, I couldn't find it. If you could get it for me and just keep it so I can have it." She hesitated. Her time with Rose was up.

The deputy got out and opened the door on Rose's side.

"I'll get it," Rose said reassuringly.

Rose patted her on the arm and stepped out of the car and headed toward the lobby. She figured that there should be a wheelchair inside. Deputy Davis headed around to where Sheriff Montgomery was holding open the rear door for Chariot.

Chariot slid out from her seat and waited. Rose brought back a wheelchair and moved it so it was right beside the young woman and she pulled herself up and sat down.

Rose spun the wheelchair in the direction of the front of the building. And then, all four of them headed through the hospital doors.

FIFTEEN

What did Lucas find out?" Rose was back at Shady Grove. She had stayed with Chariot while they did X-rays and bandaged the sprained ankle, but she was not allowed to remain with her in the county jail. Deputy Davis had brought Rose back to the campground once they started to process Chariot.

Rose was glad that the medical staff at the hospital took almost three hours getting Chariot treated before finally releasing her. She was relying on a slow emergency room and was hopeful that the extra time meant the South Dakota police had not yet left for Arkansas and that everyone at Shady Grove was using the precious minutes to find out as much as they could about the charges held against Chariot.

She knew Sheriff Montgomery had called the police in Pierre from the station to make his official report. Before she left with the deputy she heard him place the call letting them know that he had in custody the woman wanted for murder in the state of South Dakota.

Rose had tried to talk him out of making the call, but it was useless. Sheriff Montgomery was a "by-the-book" lawman and no amount of charm or begging could make him change his mind.

He had promised her that he would assign an officer to watch Chariot and that he would not let her be removed from the jail until he was confident that she was being turned over to the right people. In the meantime, he had said that he would check out the murder charges filed against her and try to find out the names of the officers who investigated the homicide in Pierre and the ones planning to make the trip to Arkansas to pick up the offender. He would keep an eye out for anything out of the ordinary that might happen.

Even as she was trying to convince Montgomery to withhold his report to South Dakota, Rose had called Rhonda from the hospital and delegated responsibilities to everyone. She had even asked Ms. Lou Ellen to help out by looking up South Dakota newspapers online to check out local police reports that might have made mention of a robbery in the state capital in the most recent months. She thought that there might be some public record of what Jason had done.

Rose knew that Ms. Lou Ellen had recently bought a laptop computer to be able to stay in touch with astrologists and that she had become quite efficient at researching information. She also knew that the older woman would love a project and appreciated being able to help out.

"He was calling some old friends in Rapid City to see if they had heard any news," Rhonda replied to Rose's question about what Lucas had found out. "But he doesn't know anything yet."

Rhonda was the only one waiting at the office for Rose to return. After Rose's phone call from the hospital and the division of responsibilities, Lucas had gone to talk to a friend who had connections in South Dakota. Ms. Lou Ellen and Thomas had left to do their work on their computers, looking up the information Rose had requested. Rose glanced through the window and could see a small light on in the older woman's cabin. She wondered if her friend was still up.

She glanced over at the clock on the office wall. It was nearing midnight. She knew that they didn't have a lot of time, but she wasn't sure exactly what else could be done.

"Did you call Lionel?" she asked, wondering what the lawyer was going to do to help Chariot, if there was anything he could do with a woman facing charges in a state other than Arkansas.

Rhonda nodded. "I talked to him before the sheriff took her into custody," she explained. "He was trying to put some things together to slow the process of extradition, but he didn't seem real hopeful."

Rose stood at the counter.

"He did have a good contact in South Dakota, though," Rhonda added. "He said she was a real good lawyer and would take good care of Chariot." She seemed relieved to report this bit of information.

"That's something," Rose responded.

"Yep," Rhonda noted.

There was a silence as the two tried to determine what they should do next.

"I've been trying to think about everything I knew about Jason and Chariot from before," Rhonda said. "I've gone through every conversation we had to see if I could come up with anything that might help us understand what has happened. But it was a long time ago that we knew one another. I think there's been a lot of change since we first met them."

Rose wondered if there was anything from the past that could shed light on what was happening in the present.

"Chariot said that Jason used to do some breaking and entering," Rose said. She didn't know if Rhonda knew that about the young couple from South Dakota.

"Lucas and I figured that," she replied. "He was a good kid, friendly and nice. He was real good to Chariot, but I could tell they were heavy in the drug scene and once that happens, you have to find a way to support those costly habits," Rhonda noted.

Rose walked over and poured herself a glass of water at the sink. She drank it all, wiped her mouth, and turned back to face Rhonda.

"Usually, a person learns handy skills like burglary or how to jack a car or how to fence jewelry," Rhonda continued.

Rose moved over and sat down at the table across from her. She wondered what handy skills her friend had learned to support her drug habit back when she and Lucas were using.

"So, even though we didn't know about the convictions Jason or Chariot had, the breaking and entering makes sense."

Rose had such respect for her friends Rhonda and Lucas. She knew that they had a rough history, had done drugs and been in prison, but she also knew that getting clean and staying clean when a person is an addict is a very hard thing to do.

"Did you know they had a little girl?" Rose asked.

Rhonda glanced up from the table to face Rose. "She told you?" She looked surprised.

"Yeah, she had a picture," Rose noted. Then she looked over to Rhonda. "Why do you think she wouldn't have told me?" she asked, surprised at the question.

Rhonda shook her head. "I just found out myself this morning and she seemed real private about it, like she wasn't going to tell anybody, like she was ashamed or something."

"I don't think it was that," Rose replied. "I think she believes she's lost custody of the little girl for good, that she won't be able to get her back ever again."

"When she showed up this week, I hadn't heard from Chariot in a long time," Rhonda explained. "After we got to know her and Jason, she used to call and ask for money or just say that she needed somebody to talk to. I cut her off when I could see that I was just being codependent with her, letting her get by with stuff and not holding her accountable."

Rose nodded.

"I told her that I wouldn't talk to her anymore until she was in some program to try and get clean. After that, she quit calling and I heard she was in prison. It's been three years since I've talked to her and even though she has a history of lying and doing drugs, I believe what she's told us. I believe she really was

changed by her baby and that she has been working the program, staying sober, trying to get custody of her daughter."
Rhonda shook her head. "I'm pretty good at reading addicts and
drunks. I think she's telling the truth."

Rose nodded. She glanced out the window toward Ms. Lou
Ellen's cabin.

"So, what do we know for sure at this point?" Rhonda asked.

Rose explained everything that she knew. She went over
every question she had asked and didn't leave out a detail in re-
laying the information to Rhonda.

"You think Jason owed somebody a favor, and to pay them
back, he participated in a robbery of a drug dealer and that he
took something from the place he robbed. The drug dealer
found out who had stolen his stuff and came looking for it. Jason was killed because he was involved and because he had
something that the drug dealer wanted."

Rhonda was tapping her finger on the table, going over the
story. "A police officer from Pierre is involved. He either is the
drug dealer or works for the dealer and he murdered Jason and
is now looking for Chariot. Is that it?" she asked.

Rose nodded. "I think that's about it." She was about to ask a
question about how much would have to be taken in order for a
drug dealer to kill, when the office phone began to ring.

The two women glanced at each other. They were surprised
to be receiving a call at that late hour. Lucas, Thomas, and Ms.
Lou Ellen would have dialed Rhonda's cell phone.

Rose got up from the table and crossed the room.

"Shady Grove Campground," she said.

There was no response from the other end.

"Shady Grove," she said again, waiting.

There was a click. She hung up the receiver and glanced back at Rhonda.

"Maybe just a wrong number," she guessed, moving back to the table. "By the way, did that camper come in?" she asked.

Rhonda looked puzzled and was about to say something when suddenly her cell phone began to ring and she flipped it open.

"It's Lucas," she said, seeing the number on the screen.

Rose nodded and assumed that he was the one who had just tried to call on the office phone and for some reason had not been able to complete that call.

"Hey," she said to her husband.

Rose listened closely as Rhonda continued her phone conversation. She looked over at the door and noticed a small canvas bag in the corner by the counter. She recalled Chariot giving it to Willie when they stopped by the tent earlier in the evening. Curious, she stood up, went over, and picked it up. She set it on the counter and began looking through it. It seemed to be only clothing. She wondered if the photo album she had promised to find might be in the bag.

Rose walked over and looked out the window on the door, recalling the camper who was to arrive late. She noticed that the receipt was gone and figured that he must have arrived while she was at the hospital. She looked across the driveway and noticed the light still on in Ms. Lou Ellen's cabin. The rest of the campground was dark.

She glanced back at the canvas bag and wondered when Willie had put it in the office. She looked out the window toward his camper, but she could see no lights on there. Rose turned around when she heard Rhonda flip her cell phone shut. "Did he find out anything?" Rose asked.

Rhonda nodded. "He talked to a biker who lives in Rapid. He's a good guy but he still hangs out with the folks walking on the wrong side, if you know what I mean." She raised her eyebrows at Rose.

Rose nodded. She headed back over to the table.

"He runs a biker bar there."

Rose sat down. She left the canvas bag on the counter to finish going through after she heard about the conversation.

"This guy said he heard some bikers from Pierre talking about some break-in a couple of weeks ago."

Rose listened closely. "Lucas get any names?" she asked.

Rhonda nodded. "I think so, but I didn't ask him."

"Okay, I'm sorry, go ahead." Rose realized that she had interrupted Rhonda's story.

"He said that there was talk that a couple of ex-cons had robbed a guy in Pierre." She stuck the phone in her pocket. "He said that the guy was a known drug dealer, a bad dude, and that was what made the story so interesting." She paused. She wanted to make sure she wasn't missing any of the details.

"All the bikers were surprised that anybody would try and rob this dealer," she continued. "He is apparently notorious for having a bad temper."

Rose nodded. "If he was the guy that was robbed and he was the guy who had Jason killed, that would make sense."

"Anyway, what has everybody talking, is that all three of the guys who pulled off the robbery are either missing or dead."

"And Jason is one of them?" Rose asked.

"I assume so. He just said the bartender had heard that one guy was found shot, the other had been in a mysterious bike accident, and the third one hasn't been heard from since the robbery."

"So, Jason is probably the one who was shot, right?" she asked.

Rhonda nodded.

"Is that all?" Rose asked.

"That's all he's got," Rhonda replied.

"Then it does sound like what we thought. This drug dealer got robbed and then went looking for revenge." Rose stopped, trying to sort through the information. "Except there's still something that the dealer is looking for, something that he thought Jason took and that Chariot now has."

Rose glanced back at the bag on the counter and was just about to get up and continue searching it when they heard the sound of gunfire coming from somewhere inside the campground, somewhere near the sites at the woods.

SIXTEEN

Call the sheriff and I'll go see what's happened," Rhonda instructed Rose. She had jumped up from the table and headed over to reach behind the counter. She grabbed a flashlight and moved to the door.

"No, I'm going with you!" Rose replied, and both of the women jumped off the porch and hurried in the direction of where they had heard the gunfire.

They both ran, thinking that it came from the back part of the campground, near the sites at the edge of the woods. They sprinted up the driveway and around the camping cabins and the Boyds' trailer to find Old Man Willie standing at the front of Chariot's tent with a shotgun in his hand. He had it aimed at the tent.

Only one or two lights came on in some of the rigs, but no one seemed to be venturing out to investigate. Rose was glad that no one else was camping in the tent section of Shady Grove.

She knew that the campers along the river may have heard the shot, but no one would have heard it as loudly as Rose and Rhonda. She hoped everyone would just assume it was a car backfiring or something from the other side of the river.

"Willie!" Rhonda yelled, when she saw what was going on. She shined the light in the old man's face. "What are you doing?"

She and Rose were spent from their run from the office. Rose dropped down, holding her sides, trying to catch her breath. She turned to Rhonda, who was a bit winded from the run but not as much as Rose. She wondered how her friend stayed in such good shape.

"He was trespassing," Willie finally replied, squinting at the light in his eyes. His words were clear and he was to the point. He glanced over to Rose, still bent down. "You okay?" he asked.

She nodded, her breathing labored.

"Who was trespassing?" Rhonda asked. She glanced around, throwing the light in all directions, and still didn't see anybody.

Willie gestured with his chin into the tent. As if being signaled to make his exit, a man walked out with his hands in the air. Rhonda turned the flashlight on him. Rose stood up and both women studied him; he wasn't anyone they recognized.

"Your guy is crazy," he announced as he stepped out. He ducked as he came through the flap, but he did not lower his hands. Like Willie, he squinted at the light being shone in his eyes.

Rhonda lowered the flashlight a bit.

He appeared young, twentysomething, Rose thought. His long brown hair was tied back in a ponytail. He was wearing jeans, cowboy boots, and a loose-fitting leather jacket.

"What are you doing in that tent?" Rhonda asked. She stood next to Willie. The shotgun was still aimed in the man's direction.

"I heard something, an alarm or something that kept buzzing. I'm in the tent in the next site," he said, pointing with his chin to the right of where he was standing. "It was annoying me."

The other three looked over and saw a small tent pitched just beside Chariot's. It was for one person, small enough to fold up and put in a backpack. His pickup truck was parked on the other side of it.

"What's your name?" Rose asked.

"Booker," he replied. "James Booker." He kicked a small rock from under his boot. "I called this afternoon," he added. Then he stared at Rhonda. "Look, can I put my hands down?" he asked. "And would you turn off that light?"

She shook her head. "Not yet," she answered.

There was a pause as the group stood waiting, trying to figure out what they should do. In the silence they heard a kind of beeping noise, low but constant.

Rose shrugged at Rhonda, suddenly remembering the reservation she had taken earlier in the day. She thought the name he gave did sound familiar. She thought that it was the name of the man who had made a reservation. Rhonda signaled for him to step aside and Rose moved behind him through the flap and into the tent. She was gone only a few seconds when she came out with an alarm clock. The buzzer was going off. She showed it to the others and then, stepping over to Rhonda and standing under the flashlight so that she could see the dials, she switched the alarm off. The noise stopped.

"See?" the intruder said. "That's all I wanted to do," he insisted. "I stood at the tent for a while, calling out for somebody in there. When nobody answered me, I thought they had taken off somewhere. So, I had just stepped in to turn the thing off myself when Shotgun Man over there came to the tent to kill me. That's all I was doing," he added.

The two women waited, studying him. Rose lifted her shoulders at Rhonda, shrugging. She thought the story was credible. There was a clock making a noise and it was kind of annoying. She would have done the same thing.

Rhonda nodded. "Okay, you can put your arms down," she instructed him. "Slowly," she added.

The man did as she requested. He turned to look at Willie. "Do you mind telling your security guard to lower the gun?" he asked. "He makes me nervous," he said with a sneer.

Willie grinned. He seemed to enjoy the attention.

Rhonda made a gesture to Willie, signaling him to reposition his weapon away from the camper. He lowered the gun beside him, but kept a close eye on the man still standing in front of him.

"This place is nuts," the man added. He shook his head. "I just wanted a little piece of ground to sleep on for the night. I didn't want to bother anybody. I planned to get in my tent and sleep."

Rose looked over at Willie and noticed that he had a flashlight in his shirt pocket. "Can I borrow that?" she asked.

Willie nodded and handed it to her. She turned it on and walked into the tent. She looked around to make sure nothing was missing from Chariot's things. She tried to recall how it had looked earlier in the evening when she had stopped by to get the young woman to walk over to Thomas's and later when she and Old Man Willie had stopped outside the tent before meeting the sheriff.

It seemed that everything in the tent was the same. Except for the purse and small bag that she had already seen with Chariot and at the office, nothing seemed to be any different than before. The sleeping bag and the pillows were untouched. There was still a duffel bag stashed in one corner filled with clothes, and the small metal table was still standing.

Rose glanced around again and was about to exit, letting Rhonda know that everything was fine, when she noticed a pink book sticking out from the bottom of the sleeping bag. She walked over, pulled it out, and saw that it was a photo album. She recognized it to be the one that Chariot had asked her to locate, the one she had mentioned in their ride over to the hospital.

She opened it, turning the pages, and saw lots of pictures of a little girl—Constance, she recognized—all dated and marked with a note. She read some of them and suddenly felt very intrusive. She then closed it. She stuck it under her arm and was about to walk out. Just as she did, a photo card, as small as a quarter, slid out from one of the album pages.

Rose bent down and retrieved it. She immediately recognized it to be a photo card, the tiny ones for the new cameras. It was exactly like the one Mary had showed her when she bought a digital camera only a few weeks earlier.

Mary had wanted to take lots of pictures of her sister while she was visiting and she had gone over to Memphis and bought a new digital camera. She was learning how to use the camera when she showed it to Rose. They had both commented at the size of the small memory card included with the camera. They read the instructions and learned that Mary could remove the card and use it with a computer to make photograph prints at home or take it to a pharmacy or discount store and use their computers and printers. They had loaded the software on Ms. Lou Ellen's laptop because the computer at the office was too old.

Rose stuck the memory card in her pocket, assuming that Chariot had taken digital pictures and that the card included more photographs of the little girl. She stuck the album under her arm and walked out to join the others. She wasn't sure if Chariot could have the photographs while she was in the West Memphis jail, but she had promised to get it for her.

"How does it look in there?" Rhonda asked Rose.

Rose nodded. "It's fine," she replied.

"What have you got?" Rhonda asked, seeing the album at Rose's elbow. She wondered what her friend had taken from the tent.

Rose glanced down at the album. "Some pictures," she reported. "Chariot wanted them." She shrugged. "I'm not sure the sheriff will let her keep them in her cell, but she asked me to get them for her."

Rhonda nodded.

The man standing at the tent seemed to be watching Rose with the album. "Well?" he asked. It appeared as if he wanted permission to leave Chariot's tent.

Rhonda sighed. "It's okay in the tent, then?" she asked Rose.

"I'd say it's fine," she replied. "It doesn't look like anything's missing," Rose added. She stuck the album under her arm. She noticed how the man seemed to be studying it. She turned to Rhonda. "I think he's telling the truth."

"Uh, yeah," the man replied, sounding agitated with all of the commotion and attention surrounding him. It was as if he had grown tired and bored with the entire situation. "Can I go then?" he asked, glaring at Rhonda.

She nodded. "Yep," she replied, still holding the flashlight in his direction. "Next time, though, Mr. Booker, that you're disturbed about a noise at another camper's site, call the manager on duty. We'll take care of it for you. Don't go trespassing into other people's stuff," she said.

"Is that your manager on duty?" he asked, looking at Willie. "The one who fires his shotgun in the air, scaring people to death."

Willie grinned.

"He's one of them," Rhonda replied. "The others carry machine guns," she added.

Rose laughed.

"Just stay out of other people's property," Rhonda added.

"You don't need to worry," the man replied. "I'm leaving

anyway. I've had enough of West Memphis, Arkansas, and the Shady Grove Campground." He folded his arms across his chest. "I'm afraid that if I stay here another hour, I might just wake up and have a shotgun at my head." And then he spat on the ground and turned and walked away in a huff.

The three residents of Shady Grove watched as he marched to the site beside them and started taking down his tent.

"You think he can do that in the dark?" Rhonda asked.

Rose shrugged. "I guess he's going to have to if he's planning to leave now," she replied.

They kept watching him and Rose suddenly had a funny feeling about him. She shone the light in his direction and she noticed the emblem on the back of his jacket. It was a white lightning bolt.

"So, what happened?" Rhonda asked Willie, disrupting Rose's thought about the jacket.

"I saw him over here and thought he was messing in Chariot's stuff," Willie confessed. "I didn't hear no clock buzzing," he added.

Rhonda and Rose smiled. They both knew that Willie was hard of hearing and often missed subtle sounds at Shady Grove. Still, Rose could see that Rhonda was not angry with her friend. He kept a good eye on Shady Grove, especially after-hours. And after he spoke up in Chariot's defense when she met the sheriff, Rhonda and Rose could tell that Willie had developed some rapport with the young camper.

Rhonda and Rose were glad to see Willie reaching out, since he was known to be a loner. Rose often worried about him because he stayed to himself so much. She was just about to ask him about Chariot, about why he was suddenly interested in this camper, drawn to this young woman. But when she looked over at him, seeing clearly the way he was protecting Chariot's property, and recalled how soft he seemed standing next to her before Chariot had left with the sheriff, she decided not to ask. After all, it was none of her business what Willie felt for Chariot.

Rhonda patted him on the shoulder. "You were just doing your job, Willie," she reassured him. "That's why you make the big bucks around here," she added playfully.

She and Rose knew that Willie got free rent at the campground and a few dollars every week. Other than that, he didn't take home any income from Shady Grove. Even though Lucas and Rhonda had tried to give him a regular paycheck, the arrangement of free rent and a few bucks was the way he liked it.

Rhonda glanced back over at the man they had found in Chariot's tent. "You reckon we should give him a refund?" she asked.

Rose shook her head. "Nah," she replied. "He was here long enough to put up his tent, that counts for a night's stay." She smiled at Rhonda.

"Willie, though, I have to ask." Rhonda turned back to the man standing next to her. "Were you going to shoot him?"

Willie dropped his head. His voice was low and confessional. "Weren't nothing but birdshot in there anyway," he replied. "It wouldn't have killed him, just made him sting a while."

Rhonda and Rose laughed. They stood outside and waited until the stranger finished tearing down his campsite, loaded his light brown pickup truck, and pulled out of the campground. The dust swirled behind him as his taillights gave a red glow down the path. It was Rhonda who noticed his license plate.

"Where did Mr. Booker make his reservation from?" she asked Rose.

Rose considered the question and saw the same thing that Rhonda had just seen. "I don't remember," she replied, recognizing the same plate she had seen on Chariot's car. "But I know it wasn't South Dakota."

The three of them watched as the truck headed down the driveway toward the main road to West Memphis.

SEVENTEEN

It was under your sleeping bag." Rose got a call from Chariot early the next morning. She was at the office after having only just a few hours of sleep the night before. She and Rhonda had said good night to Willie and then walked back to the office for another hour's worth of conversation. They had both agreed that the stranger they met was planning to search Chariot's tent, but had been interrupted by Willie.

Rose didn't have too much to go on with just his name, James Booker, and credit card number. He had made the reservation using a cell phone. She hadn't gotten any information from him except a form of payment. She planned to get his mailing address for her records when he checked in.

When Rose took the reservation she had not thought anything was out of the ordinary. Having seen his South Dakota plates, however, she knew something was fishy about the man suddenly appearing at Shady Grove. Rose wondered if he might return to finish what he started. Rhonda reassured Rose, however, that Willie would not go to sleep and that he would watch Chariot's tent for the rest of the night. Both women decided they needed some rest, so they left the office about 2:00 A.M., and went to their trailers to sleep.

It was about 7:00 A.M. when Rose got to the office and about 7:30 when Chariot called. She had wanted to know if Rose had learned anything new and if she had found the photo album with the pictures of Constance.

"Oh." The young woman sounded relieved. "Thank you so much for looking. I don't know what I would do if I lost that," she added.

Rose smiled. She had taken the photo album with her back to her trailer and even though she thought it was none of her business, she had flipped through the album pages before falling to sleep. Seeing the pictures made her consider again the possibility of having children. Rose was still not certain about whether or not she had given up on the idea of being a mother.

"She's a very photogenic young lady," Rose commented.

"Yes, and she loves to have her picture taken," Chariot responded. "She doesn't get that from me or Jason," she said.

Rose smiled. She had noticed how the little girl loved to grin for the camera. Rose assumed that because of all of the photographs the foster mother had taken for Chariot while she was in prison, Constance had become very comfortable in front of the camera. She had big smiles for every picture.

"What phone are you using?" Rose asked.

"It's out in the main hallway of the jailhouse," Chariot replied. "The calls are free if they're local," she added.

"Oh, that's nice," Rose responded, understanding how the young woman was able to call her without having any money. She knew that they had locked up Chariot's purse when she was taken in the previous night.

"How's the ankle?" Rose asked.

"It's better," Chariot replied. "I think the swelling went down," she noted. "But it's turning purple and it still hurts to try and walk on it."

"Yeah, sprained joints tend to do that," Rose said. She wondered how far Chariot had to walk. Had she taken a shower or gone to a cafeteria? She didn't know what jail was like and didn't know if they provided any assistance for those with problems ambulating. She wasn't sure if they had even let her keep the crutches since Deputy Davis had made some mention of how they could be used as weapons. Allowing Chariot to keep her crutches had not been decided before Rose left to go back to Shady Grove.

"Are you able to keep it elevated like I told you?" she asked.

"Yeah," Chariot replied. "They gave me an extra pillow to put under it."

"Good," Rose said, thinking that must mean that she was staying in her cell and probably in her bed. She hoped that meant she was safe from any harm, that no one could take her away.

There was a pause in the conversation.

"Do you think you can bring me the photo album?" Chariot asked.

"Will they let you have it in there?"

"I asked and the woman deputy said that she didn't care if I had it. She'd just need to look in it to make sure there wasn't any contraband or anything in it that I can't have."

"Well, that makes sense," Rose responded. "I'll bring it over there later today," she added, thinking that would probably make Chariot very happy. "What about the bag you packed?" she asked, remembering the small bag that Willie had left in the office. She glanced around and noticed for the first time that it wasn't on the counter where she had left it.

"Oh, no, I don't need that. It was just some clothes," Chariot replied.

Rose looked behind the counter and around the office. She was sure that she had left it on the counter when she went to bed. She wondered where it could have disappeared to. She decided not to worry about it, however, since Chariot said that it contained only clothes.

Suddenly Rose remembered the man from the night before, the man Willie found in Chariot's tent. She wondered if the young woman might recognize his name or know who he was.

"Chariot, do you know a guy named James Booker?" she asked.

She figured that Chariot was thinking about the question. She waited for an answer.

"No," Chariot finally replied. "James Booker," she repeated. "Why would I know him?" she asked.

"He was in your tent last night," Rose replied, hoping not to frighten her. "He had set up his place next to yours sometime while we were at the hospital."

Chariot didn't respond. She was waiting for more from Rose.

"He said your alarm clock went off in the middle of the night and he had walked over to ask you to turn it off. When he found out that nobody was in the tent, he went in to turn it off himself."

"Well, that's weird," Chariot responded.

"What's weird?" Rose asked.

"I don't have an alarm clock," she said.

"A battery-operated one, it's black with glow in the dark dials," Rose noted.

"No," Chariot repeated. "I don't have one."

"Hmm. Well, I did think he was a bit suspicious," Rose said, wondering who this late-night camper really was.

"It's an old trick," Chariot responded.

"What?" Rose asked.

"You give yourself an alibi for being somewhere you shouldn't be. That way, if somebody catches you, you say you were in there to answer a phone or that you heard a baby crying, wanted to turn off a radio or an alarm clock, anything like that," she said.

"I see," Rose said, thinking that Rhonda was right about the things addicts learn to support their habit.

"So, what about this guy?" Chariot asked.

"He had South Dakota plates," Rose replied. "I thought you might know him. But you don't recognize the name?"

"Booker," Chariot said again. "No, I don't know that name."
She paused. "What did he look like?" she asked.

"Tall, maybe twenty or twenty-five, long hair, wore cowboy
boots."

"Was he wearing a leather coat?" she asked.

"Black one," Rose replied. "With a different kind of emblem
on the back." She tried to remember what she had seen.

"A lightning bolt," Chariot stated. "A white one."

"Yes!" Rose replied. "Exactly. How did you know?"

"James Booker," she said. "It's Snake," she added. "He must
be one of the guys who pulled the robbery with Jason. Those
guys that he was with are in this gang. Well, it's not really a gang,
just a few guys from a couple of years ago who wanted to act like
they were tough. Put those lightning bolts on their coats. Jason
wore one for a while."

Rose recalled the story that Lucas had heard that two of the
men who pulled off the robbery were dead and one was missing. The missing man must be Snake. He had followed Chariot
to West Memphis and was looking for whatever Jason had
taken. He must have been threatened that if he didn't get it and
return it, he would be the next one to die.

"Is he still there?" Chariot asked. It was obvious that she was
hopeful that he would clear up the mess she was in.

"No," Rose replied somberly. "He drove off after Willie tried
to shoot him," she added.

"Willie tried to shoot somebody?" she asked. "I wouldn't
have thought he had it in him," she said.

"Apparently, you brought something out of Old Willie that none of us expected," Rose noted.

"Wow," Chariot said, considering the actions of the old man who had picked her up from the ditch and driven her back to Shady Grove. "That's sort of surprising," she added.

"Yeah, I'd say," Rose responded.

"Well, can we find Snake?" Chariot asked, sounding suddenly optimistic.

"We can try," Rose replied. She was thinking the same thing. If they could find the man from South Dakota and get him to talk to the authorities, they might be able to clear Chariot and get the man who had murdered Jason.

"Have you seen the sheriff this morning?" Rose asked. She knew that he was the one they most needed to contact because he could help them locate James Booker. He could help them get everything settled.

"Nah," she replied. "Just the woman deputy," she added. "She's real nice."

Rose thought about that. She didn't know that Montgomery had hired any women to work for the department. She thought about Deputy Martin, a guy she hadn't seen before, who came with Montgomery to pick up Chariot, and knew that there were a couple of new deputies that had recently been added to the staff. She wondered about the woman Chariot had met.

"Well, I expect him to come around and let us know what he found out about your charges," Rose said. "He promised to do some research last night and he should know who is coming to get you from Pierre. He's the one we want to tell about James being in town. He could help us find him."

There was silence from the other end of the line.

"Chariot?"

Still nothing.

"Chariot, are you there?" Rose asked.

"Yeah," she finally answered. "There's a couple of cars that just pulled up in the parking lot," she noted.

"You can see that?" Rose asked. She still wasn't sure that she knew where in the jail the phone booths were located.

"Yeah, I can see outside." She hesitated. "I think they're South Dakota cops," she added.

"Are you sure?" Rose asked. She glanced at the clock and figured that they must have driven all night to get to Arkansas. She was sure that the sheriff hadn't called them until almost midnight. She wondered how they could have gotten all the way from South Dakota in just seven hours.

There was another pause.

"Chariot?" she asked.

"Yeah, just a minute. I'm going to take a look."

The line sounded as if it went dead. Rose waited. She looked out the office window and saw Ms. Lou Ellen coming in her direction. She had her laptop computer in her hands. She stopped in the driveway and Rose looked in the direction her friend was facing and saw Thomas walking toward her. He was holding a stack of papers. She assumed that they had both completed their research and were bringing in their work to share with Rose.

"Chariot?" she called out.

There was nothing.

"I can't see," finally came the response. "They parked on the other side of the building.

"Oh," Rose responded.

"So, you're going to try and find Snake today?" Chariot asked. "And then maybe I'll get out of all of this."

Rose smiled. She didn't want to get the young girl's hopes up, but it did seem likely that if one of the three robbers was still alive and could make a statement about what was going on, Chariot could be freed. She could hardly believe it would be this simple.

"I'm going to see what I can do." She wasn't sure how she could find the guy who had left in such a huff the night before, but she figured that since he hadn't found what he was looking for that he would still be around the town somewhere. With all of her connections, and if the sheriff got involved, she certainly should still be able to find the guy.

"And you'll bring the album?" Chariot asked.

"Sure," Rose replied. "Oh, by the way, I have the photo card, too," she noted, recalling how it had fallen out of the album when she was leaving the tent.

Rose glanced down and realized that since she was wearing the same pants from the night before, that the card was still in her pocket. She reached in and felt it exactly where she had placed it.

"What card?" Chariot asked.

"The little digital camera card," Rose replied. "It was stuck in your photo album," she added.

There was a pause.

"I don't have a digital camera," Chariot said, sounding a bit confused. "Are you sure it was in my album?" she asked.

Rose was surprised. She felt in her pocket to make sure that the card was there.

"I'm sure it came out of the photo album when I was leaving the tent. It dropped out. I picked it up and stuck it in my pocket. I still have it." She pulled the card out of her pocket and set it on the desk.

There was silence from the other end of the phone line.

"Chariot?" she called.

Just as before, there was no reply. Rose thought that maybe the young woman had placed the receiver down again to see who was in the parking lot or who was coming into the station. She waited.

"Chariot?" she called out the name again.

She waited and then she heard the line go dead. There was a click and then a series of beeps began.

"Chariot?" Rose called out again, hearing nothing but the beeps. It seemed that someone had hung up the phone that Chariot had been talking on. Rose just didn't know who that someone was.

EIGHTEEN

Dear, to whom are you speaking?" Ms. Lou Ellen and Thomas had walked into the office.

Rose was standing at the desk, appearing as if she were on the phone. The receiver, however, was pulled away from her chin, as if she were waiting for someone and not involved in a conversation. She shook her head and rolled her eyes, as if that would explain to her friends that she was engaged in a frustrating phone call.

The two shut the door behind them. Ms. Lou Ellen was waiting for a response.

"I'm on hold," Rose finally replied.

"Ah," Ms. Lou Ellen responded with a smile. "How lovely," she added. She walked over to the table and began setting up her laptop computer. She plugged it in, turned it on, and pulled out a chair.

Thomas stood at the counter. He glanced over the papers he

had in his hand and organized them while he waited for Rose to finish her conversation.

"No, I was just talking to her." She readjusted the receiver so that the other party could hear her clearly. She shook her head again at Thomas. "Yes, I'll keep holding," she added. She blew out a breath.

"I was in the middle of a conversation and we got cut off," she explained to Thomas and Ms. Lou Ellen. "I called back because I just want to make sure everything's okay."

The two nodded and continued to do what they were doing. Ms. Lou Ellen sat down in front of her computer. Thomas was reading over the papers he had brought in with him.

"She's in the infirmary?" Rose asked. "Are you sure?" She waited. "Is everything okay?" Another pause. "Did something happen? I was just on the phone with her not more than five minutes ago. We got cut—" She was interrupted.

Thomas looked up and listened. He could see that Rose was getting flustered. She glanced at him and he winked. It seemed to calm her a bit.

"You've seen her in there?" she asked. There was some response from the other end.

"Okay, if you're sure she's all right," she said into the phone. There was a reply and then Rose hung up. She shook her head.

"What's up?" Thomas asked.

"Chariot," she replied.

Thomas waited.

"I've just got a bad feeling," she said. She rubbed her neck.

"What did you find out in your research?" she asked her friends.

"Dear, did you get any sleep last night?" Ms. Lou Ellen had turned to face her friend. She could see the dark circles under Rose's eyes and knew that she was wearing the same outfit she had on the day before.

"Not much," Rose replied. "Why? Do I look that bad?" She walked over to the table and glanced in the mirror that she could see in the small bathroom since the door was open. She still held the small card in her hand that she had picked up from the desk and she dropped it on the table as she tried to smooth down the sides of her hair.

Ms. Lou Ellen just lifted her eyebrows and went back to work booting up her computer. She noticed the small card Rose had dropped on the table and, without thinking, inserted it in her computer.

"Really?" Rose asked. She knew her friend didn't want to answer the question. "I do look bad, don't I?" She turned to Thomas.

"You look fine," he replied. "Just tired," he added.

"What time did you get to bed?" he asked.

She shook her head and walked back to the desk. "I don't know. After two, I guess."

"That late?" Thomas asked. He had not seen Rose since she had left with Chariot to go to the hospital.

"It was a crazy night," Rose replied, slumping down in the seat at the desk.

"Your horoscope mentions that a stranger comes down the

path in your direction," Ms. Lou Ellen noted. Apparently, she was not retrieving the information she had found about South Dakota, she was reading the daily horoscopes.

"Well, that must be last night's reading because having a stranger come down my path has already happened," Rose responded.

Thomas and Ms. Lou Ellen turned to Rose to hear more.

"You didn't hear the gunshot?" she asked, assuming that everyone at Shady Grove had heard Willie firing off his weapon.

They both shook their heads.

"Lester Earl did make a bit of a racket about one thirty or so. Was that it?" Ms. Lou Ellen asked.

Rose nodded.

"I thought the old dog was recalling his days as my bedmate and woke up with his manly passion, if you know what I mean." She winked.

Rose rolled her eyes. She knew that her friend teased about her three-legged companion, claiming that the dog was the reincarnation of one of her ex-husbands.

"A man from South Dakota, we think a friend of Chariot's boyfriend, was in her tent last night looking for something," Rose explained. "Willie surprised him with his shotgun."

"Well, I would imagine that was quite a surprise," Ms. Lou Ellen surmised. "Was anyone hurt?"

Rose shook her head. "No," she replied. "But the guy got away and Chariot and I think that if we can find him, he can clear up a lot of this stuff about her, probably get her out of jail and out of trouble."

"So you were talking to Chariot?" Thomas asked, recalling the phone conversation Rose was having when they came into the office.

"Yes," Rose replied. "She called me when I got in this morning and we were talking about the man in the tent and when I described him, she thought she recognized him from Pierre."

"Why did you say that you had a bad feeling?" Ms. Lou Ellen asked.

Rose looked confused. She thought for a second and then remembered her last phone call, the one to the jail. "Oh, right, because we got cut off."

"You and the man in the tent?" Ms. Lou Ellen asked, trying to follow her friend.

"What?" Rose shook her head. "No," she replied. "Me and Chariot."

"Oh." Ms. Lou Ellen nodded. "That's who you were on the phone with this morning when you were disconnected."

"Right," Rose responded. "Then when you walked in, I had just called back and they said she was in the infirmary," she added. "But I think that's odd because how did she get to the medical clinic so quickly?"

Thomas shrugged. "I guess when her call was cut off she wasn't allowed to make another one and they just took her to check out her ankle."

Rose rubbed her eyes, trying to clear her head.

"What happened to the stranger who came down the path, the one Willie tried to shoot?" Ms. Lou Ellen wanted to know.

"He got away," Rose replied. "He acted like he was really angry about what had happened and he loaded up his stuff and took off." She recalled how he stomped away from the tent and left in such a hurry. She wished that she had tried to stop him.

"And Chariot thinks she knows who it was?" Thomas asked, trying to piece together what happened during the night.

Rose nodded. "What we think is that Jason—"

"Chariot's young lover," Ms. Lou Ellen interrupted.

"Chariot's young lover," Rose repeated. "Jason was involved in a robbery of a bad guy and that Jason took something from the guy they robbed. He was killed because this guy wants his stolen property back. Lucas heard the talk around town and they say that there were three men involved in the robbery. Jason and one other are dead and a third one is missing." She went over all of the details that she knew.

"Discovered in West Memphis, Arkansas, going through Jason's girlfriend's tent," Thomas concluded.

"Right," Rose said.

"That means you're saying that if you can find this guy again . . . wait, did Chariot know his name?" Thomas asked.

"Snake," Rose replied.

"Of course," Ms. Lou Ellen responded. "What else would the name of a pillaging stranger be?"

Rose smiled.

"That means," Thomas continued, "that if we can find Snake, he could corroborate Chariot's story about Jason and perhaps clear her of these murder charges."

"That's what we were thinking," Rose replied.

"Any idea of what the stolen property is?" Thomas asked.

Rose shook her head. "That is the part we can't figure out."

The three of them thought about what the man could have been searching for in Chariot's tent.

"So, tell me what you found?" she asked.

"Well, I did read some things about the drug scene in Pierre, South Dakota. Apparently, they have as much of a problem with substance abuse in the Great Plains states as we do down here." Thomas was looking through his papers.

"I made copies of some of the articles. Most of them just talk about meth labs, how the drugs are made, how rampant the issue is in South Dakota. There's one senator from Mitchell who's really hot on this subject. It's her main political issue. Her name is Dilliard, Maxine Dilliard. There were a few people mentioned in arrests that have been made." He pulled out one page.

"Anyone named the president?" Rose asked, still trying to understand this reference that Chariot said Jason made before he died.

Thomas shook his head. "Nobody by that title in the articles. There are a few quotes referring to a drug king in Pierre. Do you think that could be the president?" he asked.

Rose thought about that possibility. "I don't know. The president, the king, I guess they could be the same person."

"Does it say who this person is?" Rose asked.

Thomas read the article he had copied. He shook his head. "Doesn't look like they have a name, just that title, the king."

Rose leaned forward. "Well, maybe Lucas can get a name. He apparently has some connection in South Dakota who knows who the drug dealers are. Somebody knew about this robbery," she added.

"What about you, Ms. Lou Ellen? Did you uncover any information about robberies in Pierre?" she asked.

The older woman shook her head. She was closing up a file and opening another one. "It appears thieving and robbing are not very popular in the capital city of South Dakota," she replied. "Other than a few television sets stolen from a pawn shop, a report of some money taken from a fast-food restaurant, and a robbery at some storage buildings near the interstate, there were no break-ins reported in the last couple of months in the entire city of Pierre."

"Was anyone arrested for these crimes?" Rose asked.

Ms. Lou Ellen appeared to be reading the articles on her computer screen. She had saved all of the information she had found.

"The fast-food robbery was apparently an inside job. The pawn shop hit was pinned on some poor Lakota Indian trying to get his dead brother's property and—" She stopped. She was scrolling down and reading what she had saved from her research. "The storage facility break-in is apparently a mystery."

Rose thought that was interesting. "What does it say about it?" she asked.

"Just that a break-in occurred sometime last month, but that the people renting units had not reported any items stolen from their spaces."

"That's odd," Thomas noted. "How did they know there was a break-in?" he asked.

"It looks like a witness reported seeing a man scaling the fence and two more coming in the gate after it was opened. He called the police, but when they arrived the men were gone and no one has come forward to report anything missing."

"Three men," Rose commented.

Thomas nodded. "You think it could be the robbery that Jason was involved in?" he asked.

Rose shrugged. Since hearing Chariot's story, she had assumed the theft was related to an individual, not to a facility that involved the property of more than one person. She thought about what a thief might find in the rental spaces. "I never thought anybody kept anything valuable in storage buildings," she said. "I thought it was just holiday decorations, old sentimental stuff, outdoor equipment, stuff like that."

"Maybe the three guys knew about one unit that had some valuable stuff in it," Thomas guessed.

"Makes sense, I guess." Rose thought he was right.

"Is that all that's reported in the article?" Thomas asked the older woman still studying the computer screen.

"There's a name," she said, surprising the other two in the office.

"What name?" Rose asked.

"The name of the owner of the storage facility," she replied.

"Well?" Thomas asked.

"Robert Lincoln," she said.

"Lincoln," Rose repeated.

"Yes, dear," Ms. Lou Ellen responded.

"Just like the president," Thomas noted.

The three of them were quiet for a minute considering this newfound information. They wondered if it was possible that the drug king, the one that Jason referred to as the president, could be the owner of the storage facility.

"So, if Mr. Lincoln, also known as the president, owned this storage facility—" Thomas began the possible explanation.

"And the thieves knew that he used one of the units himself—" Rose continued.

"And they just broke into that one facility and got his stuff, stuff that he wouldn't report to the police—" said Thomas, concluding the theory.

"Then this could be the robbery that got Jason and Chariot into their trouble." Ms. Lou Ellen added the finishing touch.

The three of them made a collective sigh. They thought they had solved the mystery. Ms. Lou Ellen started typing on the computer. She was researching something else.

"So, if we can find Snake again and get him to confess to this, corroborate Chariot's story, then we can find Mr. Lincoln and have Jason's murder cleared up, Chariot released from jail, and help make a huge drug bust for the city of Pierre." Rose seemed quite pleased with herself.

"I'm not sure it's going to be that easy to find a guy who apparently is hiding from murderers," Thomas noted.

"And is a thief," Ms. Lou Ellen added.

"And get him to confess to anything," Thomas surmised.

"Yeah, I get your point," Rose said.

"Is the only name we have for this guy, Snake?" Thomas wanted to know.

"No," Rose replied. "I had a reservation for him. His name was James Booker and he was in a—"

Suddenly, Ms. Lou Ellen interrupted her. "A tan pickup truck with South Dakota plates."

"How did you know that?" Rose asked.

Ms. Lou Ellen turned around to face her friends. "It was involved in a one-car accident on Interstate 40 early this morning," she reported. "It's listed on the city news section on the home page of my Internet browser," she added.

Rose and Thomas moved over to where she was sitting to see the headline on the computer screen.

"Looks like your Snake is dead." Ms. Lou Ellen shook her head and leaned back so the other two could read the report for themselves.

NINETEEN

The three friends looked up when the office door opened. It was Rhonda and Lucas.

"What?" Rhonda asked, noticing right away the strange looks on the faces of her friends.

"The guy last night," Rose replied.

"The South Dakota one?" Rhonda asked.

"Snake," Ms. Lou Ellen added.

Lucas shut the door and the two of them stood next to Thomas. "Why would you call me that, sister?" he asked. The name seemed to hurt him.

"Not you, Lucas," the older woman noted, shaking her head. "That was the young man's name who was rousing up the tent area."

"Oh," Lucas said. He nodded and the features on his face softened. He walked over and squeezed Ms. Lou Ellen on the shoulders.

"What about him?" Rhonda asked. "Although I must say, the name suits him. He seemed kind of wormy."

"There's a news report that says there was an accident this morning on the interstate. It sounds like it was his vehicle."

"What kind of accident?" Rhonda asked.

"Fatal," Thomas responded.

"Well, my goodness," Lucas commented and began reading the report. Then he bowed his head.

Rhonda joined him and read what was on the computer screen. Everyone waited to comment until Lucas lifted his face.

"Does it say what happened?" Lucas asked.

"Just that there was a crash. Looks like it was out of town on the interstate near the Barbecue Shack." Rhonda was shaking her head.

"Chariot knew him," Rose volunteered. "He was one of the guys she thinks was with Jason."

"The one who was missing?" Lucas asked, recalling what he had learned about the group from Pierre.

Rose nodded.

"So, what did your friend say about this group of guys?" Rose asked. "Chariot said they wore jackets with a white lightning bolt."

Lucas shook his head. "I don't know about that," he replied. "I do know that Ray, my friend who tends bar out in Rapid, said that there was talk that three guys had robbed a big dealer and that the dealer was looking for revenge."

Rhonda moved over to the seat across from her mother. Rose stood behind her.

"Did they give you a name?" Thomas asked.

Lucas thought for a minute before answering. "Lincoln, I think," he replied.

Ms. Lou Ellen clapped her hands together. "So it *is* the president!"

"What?" Rhonda asked.

"There was an incident report in a Pierre paper that said a storage facility was robbed. The storage facility was owned by a man named Lincoln. The odd thing is that there was nothing reported to be missing," Thomas said.

"It should have probably read that nothing was reported to the police as missing," Lucas commented. "Drug dealers don't like telling anything to the authorities."

"So, this Snake guy was following Chariot trying to find whatever it is that Jason took from Lincoln?" Rhonda asked.

Rose nodded. "Looks like that's what happened."

"And now the third thief is dead!" Ms. Lou Ellen summed up what the group had figured out.

"Maybe one of us should go check out this so-called accident," Thomas noted. "Make sure it was our guy."

"Make sure it was an accident," Rhonda added.

The others nodded.

"I can go visit Jimmy, find out about exactly what the scene looked like. I know that he pulled a shift last night."

"That'd be great," Rose responded. She knew that Thomas's cousin worked as a fireman for the city. If he had been on duty during the time of the accident he would certainly know the details.

"All right, I'll go check that out."

Thomas reached over and took Rose by the hand. She leaned over and the two of them kissed.

Ms. Lou Ellen glanced in their direction and smiled. She started humming lightly. At first, Rose didn't recognize it, but then it became quite clear that the older woman was humming the tune of a lullaby. Rose blew out an exasperated breath and walked with Thomas to the door.

"Mother, what is that you're humming?" Rhonda asked. She hadn't heard the astrological reading that Ms. Lou Ellen had done, the one she shared with Rose that a baby was on its way into their lives.

"Just a little song about love, dear," she replied.

Rose opened the door and said good-bye to Thomas. Neither of them commented about the song.

"I told you Chariot isn't pregnant," Rhonda said to her mother. She figured that was the reason for the particular tune her mother had chosen.

"I know, dear," she responded to Rhonda. "But Chariot isn't the only woman capable of bearing children at Shady Grove." She glanced over at Rose as she walked around the counter.

Rhonda rolled her eyes and shook her head.

"Mock me, if you like," Ms. Lou Ellen said to her daughter. "But my reading is clear. A new life is springing forth in our company," she added.

"Okay," Rhonda said. "New life is springing."

Lucas smiled. He loved the banter between his wife and her mother. He took the other seat at the table.

Rhonda turned to Rose. "Do you think Chariot can have visitors?" she asked. She was considering going by to visit the young woman sometime before lunch.

Rose shrugged. "I don't know," she replied. "I don't know what their policy is at the jail," she noted. "But if you go, I have something for you to take to her."

"Well, maybe I'll just call out there and see." Rhonda got up from her seat and moved over to the desk where Rose was standing. "Do you have the number?" she asked.

Rose nodded and pulled out the piece of paper she had used to write down the number earlier that morning. Rhonda picked up the phone and dialed. When Rhonda sat down at the desk, Rose went over and started making the coffee. She glanced at the clock and noticed that she had been at work almost two hours and had not gotten the morning brew going.

"Mary would have my head," she commented softly to Lucas and Ms. Lou Ellen as Rhonda began her conversation. "Here it is almost nine in the morning and I don't have any coffee ready!" She rinsed the pot and began to rub it dry. "And I also haven't entered in the receipts from yesterday or gone over the reservation log." She shook her head.

"What do you mean she's gone?"

Rose was at the sink and she turned around to face Rhonda. She was surprised to hear her friend ask that question.

"Who authorized that?" she asked. She knew from her conversation with Rose from the night before that the sheriff had promised that there would be no extradition until he had confirmed that it was all legal and safe.

There was a long pause.

They all waited until Rhonda hung up the phone. She had a disappointed look on her face as she turned to look at the others in the office.

"Chariot was taken from her cell and extradited twenty minutes ago," she reported.

As soon as she heard those words, the glass coffeepot slipped out of Rose's hands and crashed to the floor.

TWENTY

He didn't know anything about it!" Rose announced, after calling Sheriff Montgomery on his cell phone. "He was still at home," she added. "He said that he had found out some important information about the murders and about drug trafficking in South Dakota. He was definitely not expecting Chariot to be moved."

"So, how did this happen?" Rhonda wanted to know. She and Lucas were cleaning up the broken pieces of glass that were spilled across the office floor.

Rose shook her head. She knew that Chariot was probably in danger and that the police officer who had arrived with the extradition papers was more than likely the one Chariot had seen when Jason was killed.

"He's sending out his units to try and find the officer and the car with Chariot in it." Rose was sitting at the desk, leaning against her elbows.

Lucas finished sweeping and put the broom back in the small office closet. "Well, little sister, Rhonda and I can certainly help look," he said. "We know some back roads and a few side streets that a lot of lawmen don't know about," he added.

"He's right," Rhonda agreed. "We can take our bikes and help them search. We'll go pick up the bikes and call the sheriff on our cell phone. We'll make sure we're not backtracking where he's looking." She turned to her husband. "We can even call for our backups," she noted, referring to their biker friends in town.

He winked. "Good idea."

The two of them headed for the door.

"What are you going to do?" Rhonda asked Rose.

Rose shook her head. "I'm not sure," she replied. "I think somebody needs to stay at Chariot's tent since somebody may still be looking for whatever it is that the president has been killing people for." She thought for a minute. "And then, somebody should probably stay in the office to take phone calls from everybody."

"Well, my dear, I am happy to make my way to young Chariot's tent," Ms. Lou Ellen responded. She was getting up from her seat. "Lester Earl and I can take our places as guards. Maybe even Mr. Willie would join us with his very capable weapon."

Rose smiled. "I think that's a perfect idea."

"Okay," Rhonda said as she and Lucas headed out. "You have my cell phone number. Call me if you hear anything. We'll be out looking for a South Dakota patrol car somewhere in this vicinity." She turned to her mother. "And you, be careful," she said sternly. "I don't want another hospital trip with you."

Ms. Lou Ellen gave a compliant smile to her daughter. She knew that Rhonda was referring to the broken hip she had suffered almost two years earlier. She was finally completely healed from that fall, and like her daughter, she didn't want to reinjure herself, either. "I do promise not to try and manhandle anyone."

"Good!" Rhonda said. And then she turned and left the office. She followed Lucas out to their trailer to get their bikes.

Ms. Lou Ellen stood up. She turned off her computer and unplugged it. She removed the small card from her laptop and slipped it back on the table where Rose had left it.

"Here's your card, dear," Ms. Lou Ellen said.

"What?" Rose asked. She had forgotten that she had left it there. "Oh"—then she remembered and took it from her friend— "thanks."

Rose walked back over to the desk and had a passing thought to ask Ms. Lou Ellen to download the card when the phone began to ring.

It was Thomas calling.

"I found Jimmy," he reported to Rose. "He was at the fire station and he was on duty this morning when they got the call about the wreck."

"Yeah," Rose said. "And what did he say about it?" she asked. She was holding the small memory card in her hand. She then stuck it in her pocket.

Ms. Lou Ellen turned to face Rose to try and make out what Thomas was saying.

"It looks like somebody forced him off the road," he said.

"There were some other tire tracks, but there was nobody else around."

"Where was it?" Rose asked.

"It was where they said in the newspaper report, just off the interstate bridge, west of town."

Rose knew exactly where Thomas was talking about. She had often commented that she thought it was a dangerous curve in that part of the road.

"And he's dead?" she asked, already knowing the answer.

"Yes," he replied. "Jimmy said that he had a pulse when they got to the wreck, but that there was a huge injury to his chest. They weren't even able to do CPR," he added.

Rose shook her head. "Well—" She paused. Suddenly she heard the motorcycles leaving the campground and she remembered the other news that they had received since Thomas had left. "Chariot was extradited this morning," she said.

"What?" Thomas asked. "I thought Montgomery promised that it wouldn't happen until he had gotten all the right papers."

"Apparently, he wasn't there when they came," Rose replied. "Anyway, Rhonda and Lucas are going out to look for her." She glanced out the window to see her friends driving away. "And the sheriff is trying to locate them."

"What are you doing?" he asked.

"I'm staying at the office in case someone calls. Ms. Lou Ellen is going to guard the tent. I guess beyond that there isn't really anything else to do," she said.

"I think I'll go over to the crash site and check it out for myself," Thomas said. "Maybe there's a clue or something there that can help us know exactly what happened."

"Okay," Rose said. "I'll see you later this afternoon."

And the two of them hung up.

Ms. Lou Ellen headed toward the door.

"It was not an accident, I presume," Ms. Lou Ellen said.

Rose shook her head. "Doesn't look like it," she replied.

Ms. Lou Ellen sighed. "Well, I guess the snake is out of the grass now," she said. "I guess that's not very good news for our young girl from South Dakota, is it?" She stood at the door.

"I'm afraid not," Rose replied.

"Okay," Ms. Lou Ellen responded. "I'm going to put my computer away, grab a book and a little morning refreshment, and head down to the tent to do my guard duty."

Rose smiled. "I'll let Willie know that you'd appreciate his company," she promised. "I'll ask him to bring a couple of chairs."

Ms. Lou Ellen nodded and headed out the door.

Rose walked out behind her and pulled the door closed. She headed over to Willie's trailer to ask for his assistance. When she got near his trailer, it appeared as if he wasn't there. She knocked, but the door was shut and the curtains on the windows were still closed. She glanced around. His truck was there, but she saw no sign of the old man.

Finally, Rose looked over toward the tent section and she immediately saw him. Willie had already taken the guard position. She could see him sitting at the front flap of Chariot's tent, the shotgun by his side. She figured that he had been there all night. He noticed her at his trailer and he threw up his hand in her direction.

Rose waved back.

She thought about walking over to him, but figured she would just let Ms. Lou Ellen join him, maybe even relieve him from what he apparently considered his responsibility.

Rose thought about Willie and his attachment to Chariot. Since her time at Shady Grove she had learned that people can feel connected to all kinds of other folks. It was the kind of place that allowed for that. She had even had her own experience with that sort of unpredictable, unexpected connection with Lawrence Franklin, the man who had drowned and whose body was recovered the day she arrived in West Memphis.

She had been asked lots of times by Sheriff Montgomery and others why she was so concerned about a man she didn't know, why she was so interested in somebody's circumstances with whom she had no relationship.

Rose, however, had no answer then and still didn't. She just felt as if he was a man she somehow was responsible to, somehow related to. And since being at Shady Grove, she had uncovered a whole series of connections to people for whom she now cared deeply. It was part of the magic of the river campground.

Who am I to question why Willie cares about this young girl? she asked herself as she looked toward the old man guarding Chariot's tent. He has a right to his privacy and even if I did ask, he probably wouldn't know the answer anyway. We love who we love for reasons that cannot be explained.

Rose turned to walk back to the office steps. She opened the door just as the phone was ringing.

"Shady Grove," she said, expecting it to be Rhonda or Thomas or maybe someone from the sheriff's office. There was a moment before anyone responded.

"Hello," she said again.

"Rose," the voice was familiar, but hardly audible.

"Hello?" Rose said again. "I can't hear you," she said, hoping the caller would speak up.

"Rose." There was a pause. "It's Chariot. I need your help."

TWENTY-ONE

What is it, Chariot?" Rose asked. She dropped down in the seat behind the desk. "Are you okay?" Rose asked before the girl had a chance to answer the first question.

"I know what he wants," she replied.

"What who wants?" Rose asked.

"I know what Jason took," Chariot responded.

"What?" Rose asked. She wondered if the girl was safe, wondered where she was. There were lots of questions she wanted to ask, but she knew that she needed to listen more than talk.

"It was Snake who was at my tent last night," Chariot said.

"Yes," Rose said.

"He had him killed," Chariot added.

"I know," Rose replied. "Where are you?" she asked.

"I know what he wants," Chariot said again.

"Who?" Rose asked.

"Jason did have it and he gave it to me," Chariot said, not answering the question that Rose had asked.

"What, Chariot? What is it that he wants?" Rose asked.

"The photo card that you mentioned before." Chariot waited.

"Do you remember?" she asked.

"Yes," Rose responded.

"Do you still have it?"

"Yes."

"I need it," Chariot said. "I have to get it," she added.

"Are you okay?" Rose asked.

Suddenly, there was the sound of a scuffle. Rose heard a kind of thud as if someone had been hit. It seemed as if the phone was being taken away from Chariot.

"Hello, Chariot?" Rose asked. She was worried that the call was being disconnected. "Chariot?" she called out again.

"You Rose?" It was a man's voice—tough-sounding, unfamiliar, and clearly dangerous.

"Who is this?" Rose asked.

"None of your business. Do you have the photo card?" he asked.

"I don't know," she replied, not sure why she was lying to the man who apparently had Chariot.

"It's foolish to play games with me," the man said. "Do you have the card?" he asked again.

"I have a photo card," she replied.

"Do you know where Village Creek is?" the voice asked.

"The state park?" Rose replied. "Near Gieseck?" she asked.

"Off Highway 284, going north, out of Caldwell."

Rose listened. She had been to that park with Thomas and some of his friends for a cookout the previous summer. She wasn't sure she remembered how to get there. She paused before answering. She wrote down the name of the park on a scrap piece of paper.

"You still there?" the man asked.

"Yes, I'm here," Rose replied.

"Come to the last camping loop. I'll find you when you get here. Be here in one hour."

"I'm not sure I can find it," Rose confessed.

"Use a map," the man instructed.

"Look, I don't know who you are or what's on that card, but everybody's out searching for you. Why don't you just bring Chariot back to West Memphis and clear yourself of this mess—"

He interrupted her. "Shut up. Get in your car and bring me the card."

"Rose," it was Chariot. He had handed her the phone. "Please, just do what he says," she said softly.

"Chariot, let me call the sheriff. I can work this out." Rose was hoping that the man couldn't hear her.

"Rose, just do what he says, please," Chariot replied.

"Okay," Rose said. "Just let me think of something else," she added.

There was a pause.

"Chariot?" Rose asked, thinking that the man had taken possession of the phone again.

"Somebody's got Constance," she said.

"What?" Rose asked. She wasn't prepared for this bit of news.

"He's got somebody in Pierre with my little girl," Chariot said, her voice shaking. "He won't let me talk to her. But I just know that she's in trouble." Chariot started to cry. "If we don't get him the photo card, he'll hurt her," she added. "Please, I don't know what else to do."

"Chariot," Rose responded.

There was no reply.

"Chariot," she called out again.

"Just bring the card. And don't be a hero. I've got people watching the park. I've got a police scanner. I'll know if you bring somebody else with you or if you call the sheriff."

"Okay," Rose replied. "Give me some more time to find my way there," she said.

"You've got an hour or the little girl dies."

"Wait!" Rose yelled.

But the line went dead.

Rose stood at the desk for a minute, trying to decide what she should do. She knew that the kidnapper was smart enough to come all the way from Pierre to West Memphis to find and capture Chariot. He had found out about and gotten hold of the little girl. He had been ruthless enough to kill James Booker, the man she had seen at Shady Grove the night before, and was probably responsible for the murders of the other two men. She knew that he would see if she was being followed and if he found that out, he would kill Constance and then disappear with Chariot.

She looked at her watch. She didn't have much time. She wouldn't be able to make any calls and get anything organized in an hour. She would have to take her chances, that maybe the man was telling the truth, that if he was given the photo card then maybe he would let Chariot and her daughter go. Rose didn't have any other choice than to follow his instructions.

She felt the memory card in her pocket and walked to the door. She flipped the sign to CLOSED and stepped out on the porch and locked the door. When she turned around, Old Man Willie was standing right in front of her. She almost ran into him. Apparently, he had walked over to the office when Ms. Lou Ellen joined him at the tent.

"Hey, Rose," the old man said. He had the canvas bag on his shoulder, the one that had been missing from the office.

Rose was hurrying off the porch. She just shook her head.

"You okay?" he asked. It was obvious that she was upset about something.

"I'm fine," she replied as she headed away from the office and toward her camping trailer. Her SUV was parked beside it.

"I got her bag," he said as Rose walked away.

"Okay," Rose replied, still hurrying in the other direction.

"I was going to take it to her. But Ms. Lou Ellen said she was gone."

The old man watched as Rose made her way to her vehicle. Rose didn't answer him.

"Is it true?" he asked. "Is she gone?"

But Rose was too far away to hear him.

Willie didn't budge from the office porch and was standing in the same spot when Rose pulled away from her camping spot and sped down the driveway and out of Shady Grove.

TWENTY-TWO

Rose drove down the dirt road until she hit the main street that intersected with the interstate. Then she drove west on 40, heading out of town and in the direction of Caldwell, a small community about half an hour from West Memphis.

It was late in the morning, not quite lunchtime, and the traffic was light. As she passed the service station near the exit, she saw a group of police cars gathered off the side of the road. She knew they were out searching for Chariot and wondered if Sheriff Montgomery was with them. She hoped that no one noticed her Ford Bronco as she whipped onto the interstate.

Rose drove and tried to think about what exactly she was doing. Now that she was on the road, she considered the idea that she could pull off and call for assistance. She felt around in her purse for her cell phone and remembered that she had taken it out when she was in the office. She had walked out and left it on the counter. She thought that maybe she could take the next exit and use a phone at one of the convenience stores or gas stations.

She figured that she could call Rhonda or Thomas on their cell phones. She could even turn around and meet up with the officers who were not very far behind her. But Rose shook off those thoughts and kept driving. Nothing made sense except to do what she had already decided to do, obey the kidnapper to save Chariot and her little girl.

Rose was simply tapping into her old professional instinct; the instinct that reminded her to do only what she was told. There was no room for deviating from the rules or considering unorthodox ideas, Rose had simply always done what she had been instructed to do. She had always excelled at obeying commands. She had made a fine nurse because she never questioned authority and always did what she was told to do.

Working in the hospital, Rose had always been more concerned about following guidelines, following protocol, than she had been about anything else. She had watched some of the other nurses on staff overstep their boundaries, offer creative options, or try something on their own. She had seen some of her colleagues in school try to take shortcuts or think up their own procedures. And even the ones who had the right idea, made a fair assessment or correct diagnosis, but didn't follow the doctor's orders or the medical protocol, were still reprimanded and often dismissed. The ones who disobeyed instructions and made wrong assessments or improper diagnoses sometimes even lost their licenses. Rose understood that, as a nurse, following instructions was always the best approach for staying out of trouble and getting the job done.

She drove along, however, wondering if her willingness to follow instructions was part of the reason that she had grown tired of being a nurse. She drove, obeying the instructions she was given, feeling like she did for the twenty years she had been in that profession. She drove feeling as if she was acting like a robot, simply following orders without questioning, without trusting her own ideas about what was right or wrong. And even though she had never disobeyed a doctor's orders, never done anything outside of written or approved protocol, she drove along the interstate and wondered if this was a time when she should have done something forbidden, if she should have disobeyed her instructions and called for backup or reported the phone call. This man who held Chariot and who threatened a little girl's life was certainly no doctor or well-intentioned healer. This man was a murderer.

Still, even though she could already hear the sheriff's lecture about heading right into danger or Thomas's questions about why she didn't call him, Rose felt as if she didn't have a choice. Chariot had begged her to follow the man's instructions, to do what she was ordered to do. How could she refuse a mother's plea?

She reached down and felt in her pocket. The photo card was still there. She had what the man wanted. She, in fact, had been the one to find it. Chariot didn't even know about it. And if Rose hadn't mentioned it in the phone call that was placed earlier that day then the young woman would probably have already been killed.

She wondered if there were photographs on the card. She wondered if there might be copies of some documents that would implicate the drug dealer in some heinous crime or some indiscreet pictures. She guessed that it had to be something horrific to cause him to go to such lengths to get the card back.

She wished that she had taken the time that morning to download what was on the card because she knew she wasn't able to do that now that she was on the road, heading in the direction of the killer. She would never know why she had risked her life, what it was that was saved on that little card.

Rose considered the idea of making a substitution. She could stop along the way at a pharmacy or some store and purchase a photo card that looked like the one she had and give the guy the wrong one.

But it wasn't like she was in any way concerned with what was on the card anyway. She just wanted to help Chariot and her little girl. She just wanted them to be safe. She remembered the man's instructions not to be a hero were pretty clear. And the truth was, she didn't really want to be a hero anyway, it was going to be difficult enough to make it to the park in one hour, Rose knew she had no time to stop and try to buy another memory card.

Traffic picked up as she headed west. It was taking longer than she expected to make the exit that the man had reported on the phone, the one that took her north and to the park. Finally, she started seeing signs for the place he had instructed her to drive to and she slowed down until she finally came to Caldwell and found the exit for Arkansas State Road 284. She took the exit and headed north. She looked at her watch; she had made it to the right road in forty-five minutes.

There was only the turnoff for the park to find and Rose would have made it in time. She would have gotten to her assigned place within the hour. Rose had done what she had been instructed to do. She obeyed her orders. The little girl would be safe.

Rose watched for signs. The minutes ticked past. She drove five miles, then seven, then ten. There were no signs directing her to the park. She started to wonder if she had taken the wrong exit. Without her cell phone, she couldn't call for directions from anyone. She was going to have to rely on the road she had taken and trust that she was going in the right direction.

A line of sweat formed just above her lip. Rose kept driving north, hoping she would soon come across a road sign or some state park notice; then she saw something she had not even considered.

A small red light was flickering on the instrument panel of her Ford Bronco. Rose was out of gas.

TWENTY-THREE

Rose felt her heart racing. She knew that she had only a limited distance that she could travel once the small panel light came on. She had dismissed its warning once before, thinking she could make it twenty more miles. She had only gotten ten before the engine began to sputter and kick.

She took in deep breaths, trying to stay calm. She knew that it would do no good to panic. She looked ahead and saw the brown sign that signified a state park was ahead. She relaxed a bit when she realized that she was close to Village Creek, the place where the man was waiting with Chariot.

Rose slowed down and found the entrance. There were no rangers anywhere around and the gate was open. She pulled into the park and watched for the directional signs to the camping loops. She drove along the narrow main road that was situated high on a ridge overlooking Village Creek and then made a quick right into the campsites.

She moved to the last loop and saw a brown sedan in the space nearest the bathroom facilities. She slowly drove toward it and pulled in beside it. She glanced down at the clock on the dashboard and noticed that she was five minutes late. She hoped the kidnapper hadn't gone ahead with his threat. She hoped she wasn't too late.

Rose took in a deep breath, turned off her engine, and unbuckled her seat belt. She opened her door and stepped outside.

She could see that there was no one in the car and no one anywhere around in the vicinity. She knew that it was early in the season for campers in the Arkansas state parks, but she had expected to find Chariot and her abductor somewhere close by. Rose had also expected to see a South Dakota patrol car since someone had managed to convince the deputies on duty at the jail to release Chariot into their custody. She figured that it was a police officer or at least an impersonator who had placed the call to Shady Grove, instructing her where to come. And yet, all that was there was this empty brown sedan.

"Hello?" Rose called out. She assumed that someone was watching. She looked all around, but saw no one. She turned to the bathroom facility, wondering if someone was inside there.

"You're late."

Rose spun around and suddenly felt something slide across her eyes. She was being blindfolded. She couldn't see anything, but she felt the man tying the blindfold behind her head and she felt his hot breath on her neck.

Rose wondered if this was the man she had talked to on the phone, the one who had given her the orders. She wasn't sure if this was the drug dealer or one of his goons. And even though she was worried about herself and the decision she had made to come to the park alone, she was also very concerned about the whereabouts of young Chariot.

"It was farther from West Memphis than I expected," Rose replied.

The man threw her against her car, and she felt him give her a swift pat down.

"You act like a cop," Rose said, holding up her arms and spreading her legs apart as he slid his hands across her. Having been raised by a police officer, she had often been used as a demonstration by her father for her teenaged friends. It had been a kind of game for him and Rose had always hated it.

"Right," he responded, not amused by her observation. "Where's the card?" he asked.

"Where's Chariot?" she asked, feeling very disoriented because of the covering over her eyes. She felt the man behind her, but still she couldn't see anything.

Suddenly, she heard a voice from far away. Still, she recognized it to be Chariot's.

"Rose, is that you?" She sounded small, frightened.

"Chariot, are you okay?" Rose asked, turning her head in the direction in which the voice had come.

"Shut up."

It was another male voice.

"I think so," Chariot replied. "I can't see anything," she added. "And my ankle really hurts, but I think I'm okay."

Rose then understood that Chariot had been blindfolded

as well. She could hear footsteps coming toward her. She thought they were moving over to the car parked next to hers. She felt herself being spun around again just as she heard a car door open.

"Give me the card," the man said. He was now standing in front of her. He seemed tall, his voice going above her head, but Rose wasn't sure.

Rose reached down into her pants pocket and pulled out the small card. She felt the man moving in front of her and then grabbing it. Rose couldn't tell what he was doing, but she thought she heard him move slightly away from her and insert the card into something, a digital camera, she guessed.

There was a kind of whirring noise as if he was loading photographs. She wondered if the other man had walked over or if he was still standing next to Chariot. Finally, she felt a push from the man with the memory card.

"We're done," he said loudly.

"Is the little girl okay?" Rose asked. She was still unable to see anything. She didn't know where either man had gone.

No one answered her. It sounded as if someone was walking away. Rose tried to listen to where he was going.

"Get her and put them in the car," she heard the man by her say to his colleague.

The other man pushed Chariot toward the rear of the car where the door was opened and shoved her in the backseat of the sedan. Then he moved over to where Rose had been standing and grabbed her.

"Wait a minute." Rose fought back. "I did what you said!" she shouted. "Let me go!"

But the man yanked her by the wrist and pulled her arm high behind her back. She felt a sharp pain in her shoulder and she dropped to her knees. He clasped handcuffs on her wrists.

"Get up!" he yelled.

Rose stood up.

The other man, the one with the camera, the one who had blindfolded her, had walked away. Rose assumed that there was another car somewhere in the park. She also knew that if she got in the car with Chariot that the two of them would be in even greater danger than they were standing alone with him in the parking lot. She moved ahead with the man until she could tell that she was standing right beside the car. He turned to say something to the other man who was apparently moving away from them.

"You want me just to take them to the woods?" he called out.

"Do whatever you want," the other man replied.

Rose thought it sounded as if he was heading toward the direction from which Chariot had just come. And then she heard the sound of a motorcycle for the first time. There was a loud roar from the engine. At first it sounded as if it was coming toward them and then it was clear that it was heading away from the three of them.

Rose heard the motorcycle as it pulled out of the camping loop and away from the state park. She suddenly became very afraid of what was going to happen next to Chariot and to herself. She tried to think of what she could do. She thought maybe that if she could talk to the man, she could stop whatever he was planning.

"You work for a drug dealer?" Rose asked, her voice a bit shaky. It was the only thing she could think to ask.

"A drug dealer?" the man replied with a sneer.

"Isn't that Lincoln?" she asked, trying to sound as if she knew what she was talking about.

The man laughed a kind of jeering laugh. "That makes for a good story, sweetheart, but I set my standards a little higher than working for a drug dealer."

"Wasn't that who Jason robbed?" Rose asked. "Isn't that the guy who killed for that memory card?"

"Oh, the young lad robbed a dealer, but when he broke in the safe he should have just stuck to stealing cash and not messed with digital cameras. Once he took more than his buddies he moved way beyond pulling just a simple burglary of a dumb dealer." Then he turned to push Rose into the car. "And you ask too many questions."

Once held by the back door of the sedan, Rose quickly turned around and raised her right leg as high as she could and then came down with as much force as she could muster right on the top of what she hoped was her abductor's foot. He screamed and dropped down.

He yelled out an obscenity and jumped to his feet and swung his fist across Rose's face, hitting her squarely on the jaw and knocking her back into the car. He kicked her legs inside and slammed the door shut.

"Rose!" Chariot screamed as the man walked around and got into the driver's side. "Oh, my God!" She was still unable to see anything because of her blindfold.

Rose opened her mouth and felt the tightness and swelling beginning in her jaw. She didn't think he had broken it, but she knew that she had never been hit that hard before. She tried to sit up, but with her hands cuffed she was clumsy and unable to pull up from the floor onto the seat. The man had made his way behind the wheel and he started the car. He gunned the engine, driving fast out of the camping loop, and sped toward the park entrance. Rose and Chariot were immediately thrown against the front seat and both of them fell to the floor.

Rose was trying to pull herself up, trying to find a way to get back into the seat, when she heard a siren and immediately felt the car starting to leave the road. There was a very sharp pull to the left and Rose sensed that the car was up on two wheels, getting ready to roll over.

The last sounds she heard before they began to tumble down the embankment toward the narrow creek below the road was the crash of splintering glass, the tearing away of metal, and the scream of the young woman on the floor beside her.

TWENTY-FOUR

Rose didn't regain consciousness until she was in the trauma room of the emergency department at Caldwell Community Hospital. Her injuries were not life-threatening, but she had two broken ribs, a large gash across her forehead, and a nasty bruise on her cheek. She tried to lift her head, but suddenly felt a wave of nausea come over her.

"Whoa there, little sister," came a voice from beside her.

Rose immediately recognized it to be Lucas. She turned in his direction. "What happened?" she asked as the big man suddenly came into focus.

"You rolled down a hill," he replied. "But you're okay. Thank you, Lord," he added and bowed with a quick prayer.

"You may have a concussion," someone noted. It was a voice Rose didn't recognize. Then a woman appeared. She was dressed in blue scrubs and was wearing a white lab coat. She was a nurse or a doctor, Rose wasn't sure. She finished cleaning the wound on Rose's forehead and stuck a small bandage on it. Rose winced at the pressure applied to her injury.

"What is it with you and these bad guys?" Another voice rang out.

It was Rhonda. She stood next to her husband. Together, they leaned over Rose. Rhonda was referring to the fact that Rose had been hospitalized once before because she was hit in the head by the person who had killed Lawrence Franklin. She had also received a slight head injury when she was trying to figure out who had killed Jacob Sunspeaker, a camper from New Mexico who was murdered at Shady Grove.

"You and head trauma?" Rhonda added.

Rose smiled a bit, glad to see her friends, glad to know that she was all right. She still felt very confused about what had happened.

"Chariot?" Rose asked, suddenly remembering who was in the car with her.

Rhonda nodded, understanding what Rose was asking. "She's a little more banged up than you. She's gone into surgery. She had to have her spleen removed. But she should be fine, too."

She reached out and smoothed down Rose's hair while the woman in scrubs moved around them and finished her work. Another hospital employee came in and talked to the other one. They checked an IV line and looked at the X-rays.

"How did you find us?" Rose asked, becoming clearer about what had happened and where she was.

"Montgomery saw you heading west on the interstate outside

of town. He thought something was wrong and sent one of his guys to follow you."

Rose smiled at that. The sheriff did seem to know her pretty well. She wondered if he was angry at her and if he was somewhere in the hospital.

"Then Willie called us, said you seemed spooked or something, drove out of the campground like a race-car driver. Mama went to the office and figured out that star 69 thing on the phone and we knew you had gotten a call from a South Dakota cell phone. So, we all just hit the road until we caught up with you."

"But how did you know where to find me?" Rose was trying to understand. "The phone?" she asked.

Lucas shook his head. "He wasn't answering his cell phone," he replied. "But we did find out it was a Pierre exchange."

Rose tried to remember the phone call she had received at the office, the one that set all the other actions into motion.

"You had written the park name on a little piece of paper by the phone," Rhonda explained. "So, even when the deputy lost you when you exited off the interstate, we thought we knew where you were going." Rhonda smiled at her friend.

Rose tried to recall what had happened when she arrived at the park to find Chariot. She suddenly remembered the driver. "What about the guy?" she asked.

Lucas shook his head. "He died at the scene."

"Do you know who he was?" Rose asked.

"A bad cop, turns out," Rhonda replied.

Rose thought about the man. She remembered how he had

cuffed her hands behind her back and thrown her and Chariot into the car. A brown car, she thought, but wasn't exactly certain.

She recalled what had happened before the accident, how she tried to kick him and was then hit hard across the cheek. She remembered how it felt once the car started rolling down the embankment, the way she thought she was going to die.

"When did you get there?" she asked her friends.

"Just after the accident," Rhonda said. "The deputy drove in the park first and then the kidnapper lost control of the car, and once that happened, you went tumbling. We came up on the scene just after the car landed near the creek."

Rose blinked her eyes and tried to clear away the cobwebs from her mind. She felt along her body to see what else hurt. She raised her upper body off the gurney a bit again and felt a sharp pain in her chest. She dropped back down.

"You broke a couple of ribs," Rhonda said, noticing how Rose was trying to ascertain her injuries. "But we think that's the worst of it for you," she added.

Rose nodded. She was glad not to have been more seriously wounded in what must have been a very bad accident. Suddenly she thought about something else, someone else.

"What about the other guy?" Rose asked. She thought about the man who had taken the memory card, the one who seemed to be the mastermind of the whole event.

"What other guy?" Rhonda asked.

"The one who was in charge. The one on the motorcycle," Rose responded, trying to remember anything about the man who blindfolded her, how tall he might be or some other characteristic that would identify him. She was trying to recall if, in fact, there were two men. Suddenly, she wasn't certain.

"We never saw another guy," Rhonda replied.

"He was the one who took the card, the one who threatened the little girl . . ." She paused. Then she remembered Chariot's plea for her little girl's life, how Rose had done what she had done to save Chariot's daughter.

"What about Constance?" she asked.

Lucas smiled. "She's fine," he replied. "We called the foster mother and she said that Constance was fine, that she was never in any danger."

"Are you sure there was another guy?" Rhonda asked.

Suddenly, everything seemed fuzzy to Rose and she couldn't remember who was at the park. She thought there were two men, but then she couldn't say for sure. She thought the man who was driving was not the same man who had placed the call to her at Shady Grove, the one who met her when she arrived. Yet, she couldn't be sure about anything except the pain throbbing across her eyes and the tight way she felt across her chest.

"I, I don't know," Rose confessed, remembering that she had been unable to see anything.

"Okay, you two, I need to do a few more things to our patient here and then we're going to send her up to a room," the woman working on Rose said to Rhonda and Lucas. There were now two other hospital employees standing next to Rose. "I'll come and find you when we know which room she's in."

The couple nodded in response.

"Little sister, we'll be right outside waiting on you. Thomas is on his way with Lou Ellen." Lucas smiled and patted Rose on the hand. "They're worried sick about you, both of them."

Rose smiled. She was glad to know that Thomas was going to be with her in the hospital soon.

Rhonda and Lucas turned to walk out.

"Wait," Rose said suddenly.

The couple turned back around.

"I'm pretty sure that there was somebody else," Rose said, suddenly remembering the tall man who had emerged from the woods. "He left first," she added. "He left on a motorcycle."

A sharp pain shot across her eyes and everything went dark.

TWENTY-FIVE

She was dreaming about falling. Head over heels, tumbling and careening, and moving toward something she couldn't see. Darkness or a thick wall, she wasn't sure. She only knew that she couldn't stop heading in that direction. She couldn't stop her fall.

"Rose," she heard a voice calling.

"Rose," there it was again.

Suddenly, she felt herself being shaken and she was lifted out of the act of tumbling and pulled into the light above her. Her lids were heavy and stiff, but she was finally able to open her eyes.

Rose smiled. It was Thomas. She glanced around and realized that she was in his trailer, in his bed. He was taking care of her. She lifted up a bit and was quickly reminded of her broken ribs. She winced.

"You were dreaming," Thomas said. "Are you okay?" he asked.

Rose thought for a minute. Suddenly, her mind cleared and she remembered that she had come home from the hospital and was staying with Thomas. She had suffered a mild concussion, but was no longer in any danger. She glanced around and realized that she must have fallen off to sleep after taking her pain medication.

The sun was shining through the window and she looked up at Thomas standing in the golden pool of light.

"Hey," she said, smiling.

"Hey, yourself," he replied.

"What time is it?" she asked.

"About four," he said as he glanced at his watch. "You've been napping almost three hours," he added.

Rose sat up a bit in the bed while Thomas rearranged the pillows behind her. She reached up and touched the bump on her forehead. She could feel that the swelling had gone down, but it still ached.

"Did they release Chariot?" she asked. Thomas had reported to her at lunch that they had planned to transfer Chariot to the hospital in Memphis later that day. She had come through surgery and was recovering nicely.

"Well, it has been quite an afternoon," he said.

"Why?" Rose asked. "What did I miss?"

"Young Chariot has gotten quite a bit of good news since you fell asleep," Thomas noted.

"Yeah?" Rose asked. "Did Ms. Lou Ellen do her horoscope?" she asked.

Thomas smiled. "You want something to drink?" he asked.

Rose nodded and Thomas went into the kitchen and brought her a glass of juice. She took it and began sipping.

"No, there isn't any horoscope to be read, Chariot is being honored by the state of South Dakota for helping them make the biggest drug bust in the state," Thomas reported.

Rose placed her drink on the table beside her. "What?" she asked, wiping her mouth. "I knew they dropped the murder charges against her, that they know she was a victim like the others, but how did she assist in the drug bust?" Rose asked.

"This senator from Chariot's hometown wants to make Chariot the hero," Thomas said. "They arrested Robert Lincoln this afternoon and they're charging him with drug trafficking and with the murders of Jason and the other two guys."

Rose nodded. She knew that was bound to happen after the law enforcement officers from South Dakota made a connection between the policeman who was driving the car and consequently killed in the accident and the drug dealer they had suspected was involved in the crimes.

Rose did wonder how Chariot was connected to fingering Lincoln. "Did they find out what was stolen from the storage facility?" she asked, thinking that might have provided the evidence.

"They did search it and found out he kept a lot of drug money there. Jason and the other guys got some, but not all of it," Thomas replied.

"So what did Chariot do that helped to get the dealer arrested?" Rose asked, still curious.

"She identified him as the one that kidnapped her from jail here in West Memphis," Thomas said.

"Chariot?" Rose asked, surprised to hear this bit of news.

"Our young Chariot," he replied.

"But how did she identify him?" she asked.

"Someone from the senator's office showed her a photograph of Lincoln and she made a positive identification." Thomas sat down on the bed beside Rose.

"Someone from the senator's office?" Rose asked. "What senator?"

"That's the big news," Thomas replied.

Rose waited.

"This senator from Mitchell initiated the arrest of Lincoln based upon the information from the cell phone call that was made to you at the office, the one threatening Chariot's and her daughter's lives. It was from a cell phone that belonged to the drug dealer, and the bigger piece of evidence was Chariot's identification of the man." He reached over and slid a piece of hair out of Rose's eyes.

Rose felt confused.

"She plans to give Chariot some citizenship award. They're flying her back to Pierre on a helicopter this afternoon. She's going to be reunited with her daughter as well," he added. "It's a real big deal."

Rose considered what Thomas was telling her. It just wasn't making complete sense. Something didn't feel right about this quick turnaround for Chariot and this sudden arrest and solving of the case.

"What's this senator's name?" she asked, not sure why it would matter.

"Maxine Dilliard," he replied. "The one we read about in the articles, the one who was trying to bring down the drug dealers."

"Maxine Dilliard," Rose repeated, recalling the article that Thomas had read to her, but also thinking she had seen the name somewhere else. She thought about it, but couldn't recall exactly.

"You remember?" he asked.

Rose nodded.

"Why do you look so dejected?" he asked, thinking that Rose would be pleased in hearing the news about the young woman. He knew that she wanted Chariot to regain custody of her little girl.

"What about the photo card? Why did the drug dealer kill everybody for that?"

"I don't know. Maybe it was just pictures of people he sold to or pictures of his meth labs. I guess it doesn't matter what he had on the memory card."

Rose shook her head. There was something else that bothered her about this latest bit of news. "Thomas, there's no way Chariot could identify the other man at the park," she said.

"Why?" he asked.

"We were both blindfolded," Rose announced.

Thomas stepped back a minute, taking in the news he was just hearing. "Well, maybe she wasn't for a little while. Maybe she got a look at him before he blindfolded her. You said that she had seen cars in the parking lot at the police station."

Rose considered the news and this idea that Chariot could have seen her abductors. "But it still doesn't make sense that

Lincoln would come after her for the photo card. What was on it?" she asked.

Thomas didn't answer.

"Knock, knock!"

Rose immediately recognized the voice at the bedroom door. It was Ms. Lou Ellen.

"I hope I'm not interrupting anything carnal," she said.

The older woman walked into the room wearing a huge grin on her face. She was carrying a Tupperware container under one arm and her laptop computer under the other.

"You wish you were interrupting something carnal," Rose replied.

Thomas stood up from the bed and smiled. "Hello, Lou," he said as a greeting.

"Thomas," she replied.

She moved over to stand next to Rose.

"What's in the dish?" Rose asked, noticing the Tupperware dish that her friend was carrying.

"Blond brownies," the older woman replied. "With lots of chocolate and peanut butter chips," she noted. "Just the way you like them," she added. "Gooey and extra fattening."

She handed Thomas the dish and he took it from her. "Would you like one now?" he asked Rose, opening the lid. He held them over to Rose, who was leaning out of the bed.

"I think I need one right about now," Rose replied. "You were very sweet to bake them for me," she said to Ms. Lou Ellen. She reached inside the container and took out a small brownie. "Anybody else?" she asked.

"Not for me, dear," Ms. Lou Ellen replied. "I'm watching my girlish figure," she added.

"Yep, I'm watching mine, too," Rose replied. "I'm watching it sink further and further into my fat womanish figure."

Thomas shook his head and laughed. He took back the container, snapping on the top. "You are just right," he said with a wink.

Rose smiled. She ate the snack in two bites. She rubbed her stomach and then took a sip of juice.

Thomas pulled a chair from the corner and placed it right beside Rose. Ms. Lou Ellen sat down in it.

"And what about the computer?" Rose asked, noticing the equipment that her friend had then placed in her lap.

"Ah," Ms. Lou Ellen exclaimed. "This is for your latest reading," she noted. "There have been lots of updates since the accident," she added. "I think you'll be interested to know about the baby."

Thomas glanced over at Rose, who was looking at him. They had not talked about having children since their one conversation they had down at the river over their picnic lunch.

"Maybe I'll just leave the two of you alone," Thomas said. He smiled and made a quick exit out of the bedroom.

"I think you scared off my boyfriend," Rose announced.

"I don't think I could scare dear Thomas," Ms. Lou Ellen replied. She sat perfectly erect, opened the computer, and turned it on. She was running it off of a battery.

"Now, let me see," she started, tapping on the keyboard.

She was sitting close enough for Rose to see the screen and

suddenly, as the computer began to boot up, Rose noticed something that captured her attention.

"What's that file?" she asked, pointing to a small icon that looked like a camera sign that she recognized.

"Oh." Ms. Lou Ellen studied it. "It's photographs," she replied.

"What photographs?" Rose asked.

The older woman thought for a minute. "I think those are Mary's pictures," she replied. "The ones on her card that you had on the table in the office a few days ago," she added.

Rose thought about her answer. "I didn't have Mary's card," she replied.

"Yes," the older woman said. "You placed it next to me the morning of the accident. I thought you had received them from Mary and so I downloaded them," she explained.

"From the day of the accident?" Rose asked.

"Yes," Ms. Lou Ellen replied. "You had the card in your hand and then you placed it on the table and then I took it and downloaded it."

Then Rose suddenly realized what the pictures were.

"They're from the card that the kidnapper wanted!" Rose jumped up from her bed. She felt the pain in her chest and she suddenly fell back, wrapping her arms around herself.

Thomas rushed back into the room when he heard the commotion.

"Rose!" Thomas thought she was going to fall off of the bed. He moved over to her.

"I'm fine," Rose said, shaking off Thomas's attempts to settle her back against the pillows.

"Lou Ellen!" Rose shouted. "Can you open that file?" she asked. "Can we see the pictures?" She carefully repositioned herself so that she was able to see the screen again, able to see what was going to be displayed.

"My dear, I can open any file," Ms. Lou Ellen announced. She tapped on the computer keys and the photo file began to open.

There was a moment of complete silence and then Rose turned to Thomas.

"Well, my Lord," was all that Ms. Lou Ellen could think to say.

TWENTY-SIX

You have got to drive faster than this!" Rose exclaimed to Willie as he pulled out of the campground driveway.

He was moving at what he considered to be a quick but safe pace. Rose, however, thought he could travel a bit quicker.

"You shouldn't even be in here," Thomas said to Rose, trying to keep her from reaching over to take the wheel. He was sitting by the door and she was in the middle.

Rose had told Ms. Lou Ellen to call the sheriff and show him the photographs. He was to meet her at the hospital in Caldwell, where they hoped it wasn't too late to get to Chariot before they took her back to South Dakota.

Rose had planned for Thomas to drive her vehicle, but four days after the incident, it was still parked in the space at the state park. It was still, she presumed, sitting there with an empty tank. No one had arranged to get it back to West Memphis.

She didn't want to ride on the back of Thomas's motorcycle,

so when she saw Willie by the office, she asked him if they could borrow his truck and drive to Caldwell and find Chariot.

Willie claimed that he didn't want to surrender his vehicle over to Thomas, but the truth was that he wanted to join in the race to help the young woman as well, so he agreed to drive them.

"I'm going as fast as I can go," the older man reported to Rose, who had both hands pushing on the dashboard as if that might increase their speed.

"Willie, I know you aren't used to being in a hurry. But I think Chariot is in trouble. We have to get to Caldwell before that helicopter takes her back to South Dakota."

At the sound of the girl's name in the same sentence with trouble, Willie pressed against the gas pedal and the two passengers fell back against the seat. He whipped into the merging lane and sped onto the interstate. He pushed down hard against the accelerator and Rose watched the speedometer climb. She didn't know the old truck that Willie had been driving for most of his adult life could go that fast.

They drove the thirty miles and made the turnoff on Interstate 40 into the community of Caldwell. They were pulling into the hospital parking lot when they saw the helicopter land on the pad behind the facility. They watched as the bay door opened and a woman stepped out from the passenger's side. It appeared as if they had made it just in time.

Willie swerved in the direction of the helicopter and slammed to a stop just at the side of the fence that enclosed the pad. Thomas jumped out from the passenger's side and helped Rose climb down from the truck. They both watched a gurney that was rolled from the side entrance of the hospital and was now moving in the direction of the medical helicopter. No one seemed to see them standing at the far end of the hospital, about two hundred yards from the designated helicopter landing area.

Rose held onto the fence, yelling for them to stop, yelling to try and get someone's attention. No one could hear her because of the roaring engine and the swirling blades. She glanced around, but knew that she or Thomas didn't have time to run inside and get to the medical personnel before they took off. She was frantic, trying to get someone to look in her direction. Thomas was banging on the fence and yelling, too.

All of a sudden, Rose heard the sound of someone revving up the motor on their vehicle. It wasn't too far away. Rose turned around and watched as Willie, who had backed up his truck, headed in their direction. She pulled away and suddenly saw the fence fall in front of her.

She looked up and saw that the medical staff at the helicopter had finally noticed them. Willie had plowed his truck into the fence and was still moving forward. All that Thomas and Rose could do was watch.

"Willie!" Rose yelled, but the truck kept moving.

Finally, just as he was about to ram into the helicopter, Willie swerved the truck around and slammed on the brakes. The medical staff hurried the gurney away from the pad and away from the crazy driver who had just crashed through the fence.

Thomas and Rose waited for a minute, taking in what had just occurred and then went running over to the medical staff standing around Chariot.

"What the . . ." The woman from the passenger's side of the helicopter had moved over and was standing next to the truck. No one could hear exactly what she was saying, but it was pretty clear that she was angered by the interruption. Her hair and clothes were flying all around under the swirling copter blades.

Rose immediately recognized her to be the senator from South Dakota. Senator Maxine Dilliard from Mitchell.

"I will have all of you arrested!" she screamed and then yelled to the pilot to cut off the helicopter.

Thomas ran to check on Willie, who was still sitting in the truck, and Rose went over to make sure that Chariot was okay. The young woman was strapped onto the gurney, but she was alert and oriented and knew that the person standing beside her was Rose.

"What's wrong?" she asked. "I thought you were still injured and still in bed," she added, looking Rose over.

Rose was holding her chest and her breathing was a bit labored. "Chariot," she said, trying to catch her breath. The broken ribs made the act of breathing even more difficult.

"Who are you?" one of the nurses asked. She was holding up the IV bag that was dripping into Chariot's arm.

"Her name is Rose," Chariot answered for her. "She's the one who saved my life," she added.

Just then the senator walked over and threw herself between the young woman on the gurney and Rose. "Just what do you think you're doing?" she screamed. "Are you trying to kill somebody?" she asked.

"No, ma'am," Rose replied. "I think that's been your job," she added.

Suddenly, there was the sound of sirens approaching. The senator glanced up the street and started to appear a bit nervous. "What's going on?" she asked. "Why are the police coming here?"

Chariot lifted up when she heard the sounds. "What's wrong, Rose?" she asked.

"I saw the photographs," Rose replied.

The senator glared at her. "What?" she asked. "There are no photographs," she added.

"Yes, ma'am, there are," Rose replied. "I downloaded them from the memory card before your man took it."

The senator held her hand up to her neck and the color faded from her face.

Police cars roared into the hospital parking lot and drove through the hole that Willie had made with his truck. Sheriff Montgomery was the first one out of the car. He headed over to the group standing at the hospital bay. He immediately saw Rose and nodded in her direction.

"Senator Maxine Dilliard," he said, "you're under arrest for murder." And then he called back to one of his deputies. "Martin, cuff her and read her her rights."

The deputy appeared from behind them and placed the handcuffs on her wrists. They heard him as he pushed the senator toward the car, "Ma'am, you have the right to remain silent. . . ."

"What happened?" Chariot wanted to know. "I thought everything was okay. I thought I was going home, going to get Constance," she said. Her voice was stretched thin. She sounded small, weak, disappointed.

"We'll get you home soon," Rose assured her. "Just not today and not with her," she said, gesturing toward the senator as she was being led toward the line of police cars.

"Senator Dilliard was being blackmailed by the drug dealer, Robert Lincoln," Sheriff Montgomery reported. "She, not Lincoln, had Jason and the others killed," he added.

"What?" Chariot asked. "But why?"

"Jason must have found a photo card when they broke into Lincoln's place," Rose said, filling in a few of the details. "We think that they broke into the storage facility to steal drug money. They knew Lincoln kept a big stash in one of his buildings. But Jason must have found the card and kept it." She reached over and squeezed Chariot on the arm.

"Lincoln confessed to the drugs and the blackmail attempt on the senator this morning. He was tired of her 'tough on drugs' soapbox so he got something to make her leave him and the other dealers alone."

Montgomery had talked to the police in Pierre after they made the arrest of the dealer. "He knew who stole his money, but he wasn't the one to have them killed."

"That was the senator's doing. She found out the card had been taken from Lincoln." Rose nodded at the sheriff. She could tell that they had discovered the same things in their research. Rose also knew that Ms. Lou Ellen had told him about the photographs. "The senator knew that Jason had the memory card because she knew that Jason had been with the group that had stolen from the drug dealer. Somehow, she found out everything."

"But what . . . ?" Chariot asked, still not following the logic of what the two were explaining. "What was on the card? And how did Jason know to take it?" she asked.

"We don't know why Jason took it. I think it was in the camera and he just took it when the others took the money. Then he must have looked at the files and tried to make a deal or something. We're not sure. But he obviously found out who wanted it."

"The president," Chariot noted. "Lincoln, the drug dealer." She had heard that theory, too.

"Not the president as in Lincoln, but the president as in a senator who had those aspirations. She was trying to get her party's nomination." Rose remembered reading about Dilliard's campaign in the small article found in the paper Chariot had brought with her, the one that also had the picture of her daughter on the front page, the same daughter featured on the memory card.

"The senator's daughter was apparently more than just a scholarship beauty queen," Rose replied. "She had also been involved in a kind of 'porn for drugs' exchange."

Chariot shook her head. "What?" she asked, still sounding as if she didn't understand.

"Mommy dearest didn't want her little girl's future or her own political career ruined. Lincoln compromised the senator's daughter because he wanted her mother backing off of her drug raids. She didn't care who stood in her way, she was going to get that card."

Rose glanced behind them to see the middle-aged senator being placed in the back of the squad car. "It turns out that she

had her associate take Lincoln's cell phone. She had to frame
him to silence him. And we know that she was counting on your
testimony against Lincoln," Rose said. "She didn't want him to
be believed."

Chariot closed her eyes.

Rose noticed that it seemed as if Chariot had something to
hide.

"Sheriff, could you go and make sure that Willie is okay?"
Rose asked. She wanted him to leave the two women alone for
the rest of the conversation that they needed to have. "He
slammed through the fence with his truck. I think he may have
hurt himself."

"Yeah, sure," the sheriff responded. He sensed that Rose
wanted to ask the young woman something personal.

Rose waited until Montgomery had walked away. She glanced
up at the nurses and they moved away from the gurney as well.
They needed to go inside anyway and report to the other medical
staff what was happening.

"You never saw the man who called me, did you?" Rose
asked.

Chariot waited a minute and then shook her head. "I was
blindfolded the whole time, too," she confessed. "I never saw either of the men who had us. I only heard their voices."

"So, what did the senator tell you to make you say that it was
Lincoln?" Rose asked, finally piecing everything together.

Chariot turned away. A tear rolled down her cheek. "She said
he was a bad guy who had killed Jason and that if I identified

him as the man who kidnapped me from the jail then she would be able to have him locked up for the rest of his life."

Rose nodded. She knew, however, that there was more than what Chariot was saying. She understood that there was more at stake than just getting back at the man who had murdered her boyfriend. She waited, watching as Chariot tried to find the words to explain what she already knew.

"And she said that she would get you back your little girl."

Chariot did not respond. Rose took her by the hand.

"It's okay," Rose said softly, suddenly understanding every-thing that had happened. "If I were a mother, I would have done the same thing."

TWENTY-SEVEN

You look amazing!" Thomas had come over to Ms. Lou Ellen's cabin to pick up Rose for the Spring Fling dance.

It wasn't certain until the day of the event that she was going to be able to attend because of her injuries from the wreck. Ms. Lou Ellen, however, had done her astrological readings for Rose and decided that it was perfectly fine for her to be out in public. Rose, feeling quite cheerful on that day, agreed. She wanted to be seen with the man she loved. She wanted to celebrate.

Ms. Lou Ellen had taken Rhonda shopping in Memphis. They had gone without their friend, surprising her with the most beautiful yellow spring dress Rose had ever seen. It was perfect and she loved it. Even Rhonda enjoyed the activity so much that she had bought herself a new blouse. Much to her mother's surprise, it wasn't even black, instead it was a lovely shade of pink.

"And doesn't Thomas look handsome?" Ms. Lou Ellen was

standing behind Rose as he entered. "Well, it's just a perfect night for new beginnings."

Rose rolled her eyes. She knew that her friend still thought she should get pregnant. She hadn't had a chance to tell Ms. Lou Ellen that she had decided for sure not to pursue motherhood.

Since Rose had been recovering from her injuries, being cared for by Thomas, she realized that she was happy with the way things were in her life. She was fulfilled as she was. She had been right in her decision not to have children. She was fine with the choices she had made in her life, including the choice not to be a parent. She would have that conversation with Ms. Lou Ellen at a later time, however. This night, Rose decided, was for dancing.

Thomas had a flower for both of the women. He handed them their boxes. Rose opened hers and found a beautiful yellow rose placed on a wrist corsage with tiny blossoms of baby's breath.

Ms. Lou Ellen opened her box and found a lovely pink orchid that was a perfect match with her dusky pink spring suit. Rose helped her pin it on.

"Well, aren't we just a perfect threesome?" Ms. Lou Ellen asked, smiling.

"You don't have a date?" Thomas asked. He thought his friend had arranged for some man from town to escort her.

"Of course, I have a date." She glanced out the window. "He is approaching us now," she announced.

Rose and Thomas watched as Willie walked in their direction.

Rose was shocked to see the old man dressed so well. His hair was slicked back to the side and it appeared as if he had bought a new suit.

"I had to go to Memphis twice," Ms. Lou Ellen noted. "But I'd say it was well worth the trouble, wouldn't you?" She smiled.

All of a sudden, Lester Earl started to bark.

"It's too late for that," she said to her pet as the dog stuck its tail between its legs and headed to the back of the house.

Ms. Lou Ellen's caller lightly tapped on the door and Thomas opened it.

"Hello, Willie," Thomas said, gesturing for him to come inside.

"My goodness, Mr. Willie," Rose said with a bow. "You look very handsome indeed."

The man blushed and nodded. He had always been a man of few words. "Thomas," he said with a nod. "Ms. Rose." He smiled at her.

And then, he looked up at his date. "Lou Ellen," he said, shaking his head. "You are a vision of loveliness."

"Well, my goodness," the older woman said, clutching her hand to her chest. "Who knew you would be such the charmer?"

"Shall we go?" Thomas asked, noticing the time on the kitchen clock. The dance had already been going on for at least thirty minutes.

A truck pulled into the campground. Rose looked out the window and knew that it was the couple from Texas, the husband and wife who were searching for the woman's birth family.

They had called earlier in the day to say that they were coming back to West Memphis later that evening. They had just wanted to let the office personnel know their plans.

Rose smiled when she remembered the conversation she had on the phone with the man. He had told her that through their granddaughter's research they had found his wife's half sister and that it had been quite a sweet reunion. The woman had told them that she had always thought their mother had given birth to another child. All her life, she had told them, she had thought someone was missing from their family and that her mother had always longed for another child.

His wife had cried when she heard that, the man said. And even though both of her birth parents were dead, she had found a peace that she had never had. She had finally felt as if she had, in some odd and inexplicable way, come home. After such a long life of never knowing anything for sure about where she came from or who she really was, she had been given a chance to go home.

Rose watched the truck pull down the driveway and out to their fifth-wheel trailer by the river. She was glad that they, like she, had found what they were looking for. She was glad answers somehow flowed with the Mississippi and that peace settled along its banks.

"Let's go dance!" Rose announced and the four of them headed for the door. They all stopped, however, when they saw who was standing on the front porch. Lucas and Rhonda were waiting right outside the door.

"Did you come to take pictures of us?" Thomas asked. He noticed the camera in Rhonda's hand.

"As a matter of fact, I did," she replied. She walked in with her husband following behind her. "Mary let me borrow her fancy new camera." She held up the digital camera that Mary had bought for her visit with her sister.

"She just got home a little while ago. She's been sleeping most of the evening. I think all that family reunion time wore her out!"

Rose smiled. She had enjoyed meeting Mary's sister. They made a great pair. She knew that her friend had hated to see her sibling leave. It wasn't fatigue that took her to bed, she thought. It was probably sadness.

"So, get over there next to the window and let me see some big smiles." The two couples stood together while Rhonda held up the camera and began snapping pictures. She took a shot and then studied it, then took another.

She took a couple with just Thomas and Rose and then a couple with her mother and Willie, and then a few with all four of them.

"Okay, one more," Rhonda said, snapping another shot of the entire group.

"Hey, what did you find out from Chariot?" Rose asked. She knew that Rhonda had been in touch with the young woman since she had been taken back to Pierre and that the South Dakota senator was in jail, having confessed to being blackmailed and for conspiring to have the three thieves killed.

Rose also knew that the drug dealer, Robert Lincoln, was

serving time for his trafficking and that the man who had gotten away from the park was an associate of the senator. He, along with the South Dakota policeman, were the ones who had actually murdered Jason and the others. He had been fingered by the senator.

"Chariot's good," Rhonda replied. "They're letting her have supervised visits with Constance again," she announced. "And the little girl is happy and healthy. Chariot is doing really well. Her injuries have all healed up and she seems to think that if everything goes like it should, she'll get permanent custody of Constance in about three months."

"That is so great," Rose responded. She knew how much it had meant to Chariot to have the opportunity to be reunited with her daughter.

"There were never any perjury charges brought against her for lying about her identification of Lincoln. Nobody wanted to see her do jail time." Lucas was standing closeby.

"She's moving back to Mitchell for good. Her grandmother moved to an assisted living facility and Chariot is going to live in the house next to her mother. She said that Pierre was just too sad without Jason and she even thinks she and her mother will work out their differences."

"Well, that's something," Ms. Lou Ellen noted.

"Chariot said that she thought the two of them were finding some peace between them," Rhonda explained. "She said that now she had a better sense of what mothers do to protect their children. She said that she now understands that her mother killed her father not just in her own self-defense, but also in defense of Chariot. She understands now that her mother did what she did to protect her child."

"Wow, that's pretty heavy stuff," said Rose.

"And Chariot is even thinking that she might like to be a foster mother, take in children like her Constance and give them a temporary home. She says she likes the idea of being a mother to lots of children."

"Mothers, our band of angels," Thomas commented.

There was a pause. Rhonda smiled and nodded at Ms. Lou Ellen. Everyone noticed the exchange and understood the deep love and appreciation that the two women shared.

"And friends," Rose added. "Friends, too, are the band of angels helping to carry us home, helping us to find home, mothers and friends."

Thomas squeezed her by the hand.

"So, you're all going to the Spring Fling," Rhonda said, changing the subject, looking over at her friends, how dressed up they were, how happy they all seemed.

"Looks that way," Rose said.

"It's not too late to join us, you know," Thomas added. He was leading Rose toward the door. The other couple was following behind them.

"Well, I think my dancing days are going to be a bit limited for a while," Rhonda said.

They all turned to her, wondering what she meant.

"Why, dear, are you sick?" Ms. Lou Ellen asked, looking very concerned about her daughter's welfare.

"A little," she replied. "Mostly in the mornings," she added.

"What?" Rose asked. She was still a nurse at heart. And she was concerned about Rhonda's health.

"Yes," Rhonda replied. "Mother, your horoscope readings were, in fact, correct, just off a bit."

"What do you mean?" Ms. Lou Ellen asked, not following her daughter's line of conversation.

"I mean that you were right. New life is springing forth at Shady Grove."

Everyone looked at Rhonda and then at Lucas, who was beaming like a proud father.

"I'm pregnant!"

The room fell silent and then exploded into a loud celebration. And even before they made it to the Elks Lodge, the dancing had already begun at Shady Grove.